MOUNTAIN MAN

THE SMITH BROTHERS #1

SHERILEE GRAY

Cover Design: Cover Couture

Photos (c) Shutterstock

Photos (c) Depositphotos

www.bookcovercouture.com

1

BIRDIE

I WAS GOING TO DIE.

My teeth started chattering harder.

The snow wasn't just under me now, it was settling on me. The voices of my hiking group, calling my name, had long since faded. Now all I could hear was the wind whistling through the trees, though, with the way it had picked up, it was more like a banshee scream.

The weather report said it would be fine over the weekend, clear and cold, but perfect for a winter hike into the mountains. The weatherman had been wrong. This wasn't fine, this was a full-on blizzard.

And now I was going to die.

This was what I got for trying to make friends. For trying something new. I was used to being alone; I had been most of my life. Which was why working in the Eaglewood library, since I'd moved to the small Colorado town six months ago, worked for me. It wasn't exactly a hub of social activity. Why I'd suddenly decided I needed to get out and meet new people was beyond me right then. And hiking of all things. What had I been thinking?

Tears stung my eyes. *What was I going to do?* I'd stopped feeling my hands and feet a while ago and I was pretty sure I was minutes away from hypothermia. Not feeling my extremities was the only good thing to come of this. At least my throbbing sprained ankle was only a memory.

Maybe I could walk on it? They always said to stay in one place if you got lost, but I'd been sitting there, waiting for what felt like forever, and no one had come for me. I needed to find shelter, somewhere less exposed.

Mind made up, I clung to the tree beside me and tried to drag myself to my feet. A scream tore from my throat when I tried to put weight on my ankle, and I fell back to the ground.

Okay, maybe I wasn't as numb as I thought. Black shadows hovered at the edge of my vision. I was going to pass out.

What was that?

There was a speck in the distance, but it seemed to be coming closer? No, my eyes were playing tricks on me. The shadows started to close in as I watched the speck get bigger, until it wasn't a speck anymore.

It was a...

Yeti.

I screamed, or at least I thought I did. I needed to run, but my body refused to obey me, or even move. The shadows grew darker, narrowing my vision to a pinprick. The yeti was a few feet from me now and I struggled to remain conscious. It reached for me...

Everything went dark.

My brain, my limbs, felt sluggish and I couldn't open my eyes.

I was warm, though, so warm my cheeks felt hot. I tried to open my eyes again, but it was a serious struggle, so I stopped trying for the moment. I lay still, letting the neurons in my brain try to fire back to life. It took a while, but slowly the haze started to clear. With my eyes closed my other senses had kicked in. Something smelled amazing—earthy, musky, woodsy. I couldn't work out exactly what it was. There was a soft crackling—an unmistakable comforting sound. A fire.

I'd been found. Someone had rescued me.

I burrowed deeper, deciding that opening my eyes was no longer a priority. I was safe. I was warm. I was alive.

I tried to move my foot, which throbbed dully, to assess the damage, but it was being held by something.

That's when my brain snapped back to full consciousness.

There was something big and hot wrapped around me. My fingers flexed against what I realized was a chest, a hairy one. The something was male, and that male was...

Naked.

Huge arms were wrapped around me and my feet were trapped between what I could only assume were solid, hairy calves.

Oh God.

I was naked as well.

My eyes snapped open.

My vision was filled with a wide, bare chest, with dark hair covering bulging pecs. I shoved, and the human bear surrounding me grunted but didn't release me. I tilted my head back, about to scream, but realized he was asleep. I pressed my lips together and bit back my shriek. Waking him was the last thing I wanted to do.

His head was tilted down, like he'd been watching me when he fell asleep. Short, thick black lashes rested against his cheeks and he had a thick beard covering the lower half of his face. I couldn't see much more.

I glanced around. I was in a basic log cabin, the open fire blazing on the other side of the room, and furs on the floor. There were guns leaning against the wall by the door, which was secured with a long, thick piece of lumber that I didn't think I'd be able to lift even if I could escape my human manacles.

The arm around me was a dead weight. I couldn't move it. Tears started filling my eyes as panic set in.

Maybe if I slid out from under his arm?

I started sliding downward...

His eyelids snapped open and vibrant blue eyes locked on me.

I screamed, tried to jerk back, and when those monster arms didn't let me go, screamed some more.

The huge man's eyes went wide, then he jolted, released me, and shot out of bed so fast you'd think I was the one who'd stripped *him* naked and crawled in bed *with him*.

He stood several feet away, hand up, like he was warding me off, or maybe trying to put me at ease? I wasn't sure how that was possible since I was *naked* and moments ago he'd been pressed up against me while I was unconscious.

"Who the hell are you and what am I doing here?" I watched as what I could see of his face turned pink.

"Found you..." he said in a voice that was so deep I was sure the ground quivered beneath us. "Unconscious. I brought you here."

I scrambled up the bed, taking the covers with me, and

thanked God when I realized I still had panties on, even as fear coiled tight in my belly. "Why the hell did you take my clothes off? What did you do to me?"

His brows lowered. "Do?"

I clutched the covers tighter to my chest. "I'm practically *naked*, and you were all over me."

He took an abrupt step back, his heavy brows now shooting up, eyes widening, in what I could only describe as alarm. "Woman, you were close to death. Only way to warm you back up quick was body heat."

I'd heard of people doing that before, hadn't I?

I took him in.

The yeti.

He was the giant fur-covered beast walking toward me through the snow before I passed out.

My eyes dropped before I could stop them.

Good God, he was huge.

I'd never seen a man like the one in front of me in all my life. He was taller than the door he was standing in front of, massive everywhere—thick, sold thighs dusted with dark hair, long legs, bulging calves. His chest and shoulders were wide, his waist thick, his stomach roped with muscle. One of his biceps was easily as big as one of my thighs, and that was saying something, since I wasn't at all what you would call petite. My gaze slid back down. One of his enormous hands was covering his groin, or trying to anyway.

He made a low, broken sound, and my eyes shot back up to his. His face wasn't pink anymore; it was fire-engine red.

"Can you...ah, put some clothes on, please?" My voice came out as a raspy whisper.

He jolted again, like he only just realized he was standing there completely naked. He turned away, flashing a spectacular pair of muscular butt cheeks before snatching up a pair of pants and pulling them on. The fact that I could even contemplate the attractiveness of his butt was insane given the circumstances. I obviously hadn't fully recovered from my ordeal.

He turned back but said nothing for several seconds, staying all the way on the other side of the room. I watched his jaw work, his fingers curling and uncurling at his sides.

Finally, he shook his head, his shaggy black hair falling around his face, strands catching on his beard, and leveled me with his blue eyes. "I didn't touch you...I would never..." He lifted a hand, motioning toward me. "You needed warming. I did what I needed to."

Now that he wasn't naked anymore, or wrapped around me like a hibernating bear, he wasn't quite as threatening, especially with the way he kept blushing, which was completely at odds with his size and fierce appearance.

"Can I have my clothes?" I said, feeling uncomfortable sitting there practically naked in this complete stranger's bed.

He grunted, turned to a scarred wooden chest of drawers, and pulled something out. He motioned to a rack above the fire, where my clothes were draped. "They're still wet," he said. "Wear this."

He threw something toward me and it landed on the bed. I picked it up. A red and black oversized flannel shirt. "Thank you." I stared at him and he stared back, saying nothing. "Can you, um...can you turn around, please?"

He blushed again and spun away.

Not that it wasn't anything he'd already seen, considering he'd stripped me bare and put me in his bed, but still. I took a moment to assess my body's aches and pains. The only place I was feeling any pain was my ankle. Everywhere else felt...untouched.

God, this man had saved my life and I'd accused him of molesting me in my sleep. I slipped on his shirt and quickly did up the buttons. I glanced up at the rack above the fire. My sports bra hung up there. I wasn't exactly lacking in the chest area, in fact, I wasn't lacking in any areas. Letting the girls swing free wasn't something I had the luxury of doing. I'd been big pretty much all my life. Thankfully, I'd been blessed with my mother's hourglass figure, but I was all boobs, butt, and thighs, and lots of all three. I'd given up trying to change my body, and I'd stopped hating it a long time ago. I glanced up at the clothing rack. But, man, I wanted my bra.

"I'm covered up."

He grunted, moved to the fire, and threw another log into the flames. "Stay under the covers. It's warmer under the furs."

He didn't look at me while he said this, kept his wide, muscled back to me. "So, you...you live here?" I asked.

He shook his head. "Hunting cabin."

I didn't know this man, but maybe if I knew some more about him I might feel a little less nervous about being there alone with him. "You live in town?"

He shook his head again. "Nope."

Okay. "Are you on a hunting...um, vacation?"

He picked up a pot and banged it down on the hot plate over the fire. "Live farther down the mountain."

"So why do you come up here if you—"

"I don't go to town. Don't like people. Don't like strangers. I also don't like being asked a bunch of questions."

I bit my lip.

I'd heard of people who lived on the mountain, who barely ventured to town except to get supplies every few months. Mountain Men, people called them. Men who had, for different reasons, chosen to live solitary lives

I curled my fingers into the covers. “When can I go home?”

He grumbled under his breath. “Blizzards hit. Covered everything in at least fifteen inches of fresh snow. Woman, you’re not going anywhere, not till some of it melts.”

My whole body tensed. “What?”

“You’re stuck here, and seeing as the snow’s still falling and doesn’t look like it’s gonna let up anytime soon, I’d say for a while.”

“What?” I said again, or rather choked.

“You’re not going anywhere on that ankle anyway, not until you can put weight on it.”

I could only see his profile, but from what I could see of his face, his expression said loud and clear that he was about as happy about me being there as I was. He glanced at me and his blue gaze hit mine, then dropped, lingering on my chest. He quickly turned away and started chopping a big slab of meat. I stared at him, not sure what to say, what I could do. People would be worried about me. The hiking group I’d come with probably thought I was dead.

“Do you have a phone?”

“No.”

The hopelessness of my situation sunk in, and my nose started to sting, and tears filled my eyes. I bit my lip, trying to swallow the helpless sob crawling up my throat, but failed.

He jerked around at the sound, and when he looked at me his eyes widened, and he took a step back like he’d been confronted with his worst nightmare. For some men, I guessed that’s exactly what a crying woman was. Especially a complete stranger.

"I'm s-sorry," I said between shuddering breaths. "This whole thing…it's been a little…stressful…a-and p-people will be so worried." I blinked, and tears ran down my cheeks. I dashed them away but more replaced them instantly.

My reluctant rescuer rubbed his giant hands down the fronts of his pants. "Ah…" he said.

"I'm sorry," I said again.

He grabbed a mug and I watched him put cocoa and sugar in it, then pour some milk-like liquid from a tin. He topped it up with boiling water from another pot on the hot plate above the fire and brought it to me. I stared up at him.

"Cocoa," he said and held it out.

"Oh. Thank you."

He stood there, not moving, still looking down at me. "Drink," he finally said.

I thought I better do as he ordered, and lifted the mug, taking a sip. His heavy stare hadn't left my face, but it dropped to my mouth, not leaving when I lowered the mug.

"This is delicious." I licked my lips self-consciously.

His nostrils flared, and he quickly turned away and went back to chopping meat.

My belly did a weird little flip and I sat there trying to process what it was as I watched him dump his handiwork into the pot. The sizzle of meat hitting the heat filled the air. Vegetables came next, followed by water and seasoning.

He kept his eyes averted throughout this.

Finally, he walked to a shelf, pulled down a tin box, and walked toward me. "I need to wrap your ankle," he said.

"Oh…no, it's fine."

He frowned. "It's not."

He was definitely a man of few words.

I started shaking my head, but he ignored me and

flicked back the quilt covering my throbbing ankle. I gasped. It was swollen and bruised. No wonder it hurt like hell.

He'd shoved the covers back with force and my bare legs were completely exposed to mid-thigh. He dropped to his knees, and they cracked, loud in the silence. The man was even huge kneeling on the floor. The bed was low, and he still topped me by a head.

He opened the box and pulled out a large brown glass bottle. "This shit stinks, but it'll help the swelling and bruising to go down faster."

"What is it?"

"Family remedy," he muttered and opened the lid.

"Good God," I cried when it hit me. "That is the worst thing I've ever smelled."

He shrugged. "The stink dies down once it's on the skin and heats up."

"Right." I watched him scoop out some thick yellowish cream, and before I could offer to do it, his huge hand was on me. Rough-skinned but gentle fingers working it cautiously over my ankle.

I sucked in a breath, as what felt like small electrical currents travelled up my leg. "It feels warm."

He didn't answer. I looked from my ankle to his face and sucked in another breath, this one for another reason. Those nostrils were flared again, and his eyes were following his fingers. I watched his gaze go higher to the apex of my thighs, then dart back.

I squeezed my thighs together. This was humiliating.

His face darkened again, and he jerked his hands away, roughly grabbing a wrapped bandage from the box.

"Just gonna wrap it, then I'll be done."

He worked quickly, but was still gentle, making the bandage firm but not too firm. He taped the end down and quickly threw everything back in the box and moved back to the other side of the room like I carried a contagious disease.

I tugged the covers back into place. "Thank you...um..." I realized I didn't know his name.

"Hank," he muttered. "Hank Smith."

Hank. It suited him. "Thank you, Hank. For this." I motioned to my foot. "And for carrying me to safety. If it wasn't for you I'd be..." Dead. This man might not like strangers, might prefer his own company, but my weariness was fast evaporating with each passing minute. He'd done nothing to make me think he intended to hurt me, and it wasn't like he hadn't had opportunity. For the time being I was stuck there, and Hank was the only thing protecting me from what lay beyond that cabin door. "Anyway, I'm Birdie. Birdie Winters. Thank you for saving my life. What you did was amazing, and I owe you."

"It was nothing," he said, looking uncomfortable.

"It wasn't nothing. God, how far did you have to carry me?"

He shrugged his big shoulders. "Four, maybe five miles."

My mouth dropped open. "Five miles?"

He shrugged again.

"How did you...I mean, I'm no lightweight...how did you carry me that far?"

He frowned, an expression that said he thought what I was saying made no sense. "I've carried deer more than twice the size of you." Then he turned away again—like what he said was a full explanation, and his feat of immense strength was nothing—and stirred his stew. Which was starting to smell amazing, its rich aroma filling the small cabin.

"What kind of name is Birdie?" he asked suddenly, back still to me, his deep voice making my lower belly quiver.

"Well, it's a family name. My grandmother was named Birdie."

He grunted again.

I opened my mouth to say something and my stomach growled. Loudly.

His head swiveled on his thick neck, eyes coming back to me, and I couldn't be sure, but I thought I saw his lips twitch behind that thick beard. No, I was sure of it, because his eyes lit up as well.

And the effect was breathtaking.

2

HANK

I WAS TRYING to ignore her, but it wasn't working.

Throughout my life, I'd turned ignoring people into a fine art. Now no one bothered me, accept for my twin brother, Beau.

But the woman behind me…

Images of her near-naked body fired through my mind. I felt my face heat again and willed my body to calm the hell down. What kind of sick asshole got hard over an unconscious woman? A woman who would probably be dead if I'd found her even fifteen minutes later.

I had.

I'd tried not to look as I'd stripped her bare, as I'd pulled off her wet clothes as quickly as I could, and put her in my bed. I'd done the only thing I knew to warm her up. I used my body. But as soon as her soft, full curves had pressed against mine, the fucker between my legs had swelled and stiffened until I was in pain.

Guilt had socked me in the gut. Disgusted with myself over my reaction to a defenseless woman.

Thank the Lord she hadn't woken up when I was in that

state. She was scared enough of me as it was. Most women were. Not that I'd encountered many. My face heated again when I thought about the one time I had. The fumbling overeager rutting that was over too fast with the only woman I'd touched intimately. Fifteen minutes of humiliation, arranged by my grandfather on my nineteenth birthday.

I shoved that thought away, grabbed a bowl, and ladled in some stew. I might suck at conversation—hell, at everything when I wasn't solo—but I could at least feed her and keep her warm. I had plenty of meat and vegetables, flour, eggs. Enough supplies to last a few weeks if we were snowed in that long.

The thought had me fumbling with the spoon I'd just picked up.

Another gut punch, only this time it wasn't guilt that caused it, it was something else, something I had no right even thinking about, but when I turned to her, dressed in my shirt, sitting in my bed, it was all I could think about.

Birdie was the most beautiful woman I'd ever seen.

I dumped the spoon in the bowl, strode over, and handed it to her.

She smiled up at me. "Thank you, this looks and..." She breathed in deep. "Smells amazing."

Her fingers brushed mine as she took it, and just like when I put my grandpa's ointment on her leg, zaps of pleasure shot up my arm. I jerked my hand back, retreating a step. "It's just stew."

She was blinking up at me like a baby owl. All innocent and soft, and in that moment, I hated how difficult this was for me. Beau would already have had Birdie charmed. Women flocked to him. I just had to look at Birdie and I frightened her.

And since we were identical twins, I knew it wasn't my looks that freaked her out, it was just...me. Though, I guess, I was bigger than my brother. My size did sometimes disconcert people.

"My grandpa used to say God used extra fertilizer when he made me," I said, attempting to put her at ease. Maybe make her smile?

Instead, her mouth opened and closed, and opened again. "Ah...he did?"

Christ, what the hell was I doing? She had to think I was crazy. I shoved a hand through my hair. Why the hell was I even trying? I'd been in the company of a beautiful woman for only a few hours—and most of that time she'd been unconscious—and I was already acting like a fool. "Let me know if you want more." I motioned to her bowl. "There's plenty."

She nodded, finished chewing her mouthful, and asked, "Your grandpa? Are you close?"

With her eyes on me like that, my pulse started to race a little faster. "He passed some years ago."

"I'm sorry," she said.

They weren't just words. I could see she actually meant them. "Yeah, we were close. He brought me and my twin brother up."

Her gaze dropped lower, and I felt it like she'd run her hands down my chest. "There's two of you?"

That's all it took, her eyes on me like that, and my cock started to swell. I didn't have much cause to talk to women. I only saw people when I went into town every couple of months. And besides that one humiliating encounter, I made do with my fantasies and my fist.

I'd never seen a woman like Birdie in the flesh, only in

those fantasies. She was curvy, rounded hips, soft belly, smooth skin, and big soft—

I quickly dragged a chair out at the table and sat my ass in it to hide what was going on in my pants. I cleared my throat. "Yeah. Same height, but he's not quite as...large as me."

A small smile curled her lips and my racing pulse started to beat even faster.

"Ah, so that's why your grandpa said God used extra fertilizer?"

My face felt hot again, and I was glad I had my beard to cover most of it. How many twenty-seven-year-old men blushed just because they were talking to a pretty woman? "Yeah."

She chewed and swallowed another mouthful. "Have you lived up here, on these mountains, all your life?"

I shifted in my chair and nodded.

Her head tilted to the side, exposing more of her delicate neck. "What about your brother?"

I didn't like answering a lot of questions, mainly because I didn't like talking. Talking meant interacting with people. I couldn't avoid Birdie—we were stuck together for the next week at least—so I guessed I could answer her questions if it made her feel more at ease, and I assumed by her smiles, it was.

"He left for a while, missed it, now spends part of the year up here, part working on a ranch just out of town."

Her dark brown, wavy hair had slid to one side, and her big brown eyes were still on me, wide and so pretty I had trouble looking directly at them. "And you chose to stay behind?" she asked.

I had to clear my throat again to speak. "Gramps needed someone to stay and help out." I shrugged, not touching the part about how tough those years were, how much I'd missed my brother, and how helpless I'd felt when my grandfather got sick.

Those big brown eyes turned sad. "You must have missed him."

I couldn't answer. That look in her eyes made my gut tighten in a way I didn't like. That was enough talking for now. I climbed to my feet and got busy dishing myself up some dinner. At least the topic of conversation had succeeded in taking away the heavy ache behind my zipper. I stayed standing, leaned over the short wooden bench I'd put in last summer, and shoveled my food down, trying not to look at her again. I heard movement, but didn't look up.

There was a crash, then she cried out.

I spun around to find Birdie on the floor, her empty bowl and spoon on the ground beside her. I stared down at her in shock. "Are you hurt?"

"No, not really, but I guess I put too much weight on my ankle," she said with a wince.

I strode over, trying not to look at her legs or the way my shirt had ridden higher, exposing her soft, pale thighs.

Jesus Christ.

I swallowed audibly.

I could see the thin scrap of lemon yellow fabric that covered the soft heat between those lovely thighs. Beau used the term *pussy* to describe that part of a woman, and I suddenly understood why. I'd never wanted to stroke anything more in my life.

I'd tried not to look at her panties when I'd undressed her, and failed. It was only for a second, and I felt terrible for doing it, but knowing what that innocent-looking article of clothing covered, it did things to me.

I had the strong and sudden urge to drop to my belly,

crawl closer, and bury my face against her. Smell her, taste her.

My mouth watered.

I shoved my arms under her knees and behind her back and lifted her into bed again. “Don’t move from this bed again without my help. Your ankle looks worse than it is, but it won’t get better if you pull shit like that again.”

Her eyes dropped to her hands that were pulling the covers back over her, and I watched her throat work. “You’re right. That was, that was stupid of me.”

I frowned. “Not stupid.” I shook my head. “Just...be careful.” I felt like shit for barking at her, but I didn’t know what to say, so I shoved my feet in my boots and pulled on my jacket. It was still snowing outside, and I needed to make sure we didn’t get completely buried. “I need to shovel some snow, get wood.”

“Okay,” she said softly.

I stood there for several seconds longer, not sure what to say. In the end all I managed was a grunt then I stomped to the door and headed outside.

I stayed out there until my hands and feet were numb, and then came back in with a load of wood for the fire, enough to get us through the night.

I shut the door behind me and pulled up short.

Birdie was on her back, one hand up by her face, the other on her belly. Her hair was spread across my pillow and her cheeks were rosy from the fire. My gaze dropped to her lips. They were puffy, fuller, like she’d been biting them.

I quickly looked away, walked to the fire, and dumped the wood as quietly as I could on the hearth. But when I straightened, I couldn’t stop myself from looking back.

What would those lips taste like, feel like against mine?

I slammed my eyes shut and looked away again.

The sooner I could get her off my mountain, the better.

Birdie

I woke with a start and it took me a few seconds to work out where I was. Then it all came rushing back to me. The hike, getting lost...Hank.

I sat up in bed quickly and looked around. I was alone. But I had no time to contemplate Hank's whereabouts because I also needed to pee so bad I thought my bladder might actually explode. My gaze flew around the room, looking for another door, a bathroom. There was no other door. The room was made up of a small area that was used as living, bedroom, and kitchen. There was a rustic, scarred wooden table and three chairs, a double bed, and various shelves, racks, and cupboards.

No bathroom.

And if I didn't relieve myself in the next few minutes, I was going to actually pee in Hank's bed. I shoved the covers back, and remembering my ankle this time, did my best not to put any weight on it and half hopped, half stumbled across the cabin.

Peeing out in the open, where there could be bears and mountain lions, in freezing conditions did not sound fun, but neither did humiliating myself. I grabbed a cable-knit sweater that was hanging over the back of one of the kitchen chairs and shoved it over my head. It dropped down below my knees, giving me decent coverage. Doing the same hop/stumble routine, I made it to the door and grabbed the handle—

"Where'd you think you're going?"

I jumped at that impossibly deep voice and spun on my

good leg toward the fire. Hank was lying on the fur rug in front of the fire, up on one elbow, watching me. The single woolen blanket covering him slipped, falling away to reveal his bare chest.

I blinked, mesmerized by the sheer muscled expanse of it...of him. "I, ah...I need to use the bathroom."

Hank climbed to his feet instantly. "I'll take you."

"No...I'm fine. Really, just point me in the right direction."

"It's not safe and there's no way you'll get there on that ankle."

The idea of him coming with me *to pee* was humiliating. "Hank..."

"Boots," he rumbled.

Crap. I looked down and saw my boots by the door. Right. Bare feet were probably not a great idea if I was hoping to avoid frostbite. I tried to slide my injured foot into one and winced when pain shot through my ankle. There was no way I was getting that on. Now what?

Hank strode to the bed, jerked a drawer open in the dresser beside it, and pulled something out, then was moving toward me.

He dropped to his knees, grabbed my injured leg in one hand, and I watched as he slid on a thick knitted sock.

I blinked down at him. "I don't think socks will help."

He ignored me and did the same with the other foot.

I opened my mouth again to speak, but my words were swallowed by a gasp when he swung me up into his arms, shoved his feet in his own boots, opened the door, and walked out, *shirtless*, into the snow.

He stomped through the fresh powder to a little shed that I discovered was an outhouse when he pushed open the door.

He placed me back on my feet. "I'll wait out here."

"Right, thanks." I was still trying to get my heart rate back under control after being held in his arms, cradled against his massive bare chest, as the door shut.

Thankfully, there was moonlight streaming through a cutout on the back wall. It was freezing, and the floor was covered in snow that had made it inside. It soaked through my socks. I quickly did my business and was shivering so hard my teeth were clattering together by the time I opened the door. Hank scooped me up again and stomped back toward the cabin. The wind whistled around us and the snow, which was still falling, stuck to our hair and Hank's beard.

Even after standing out in the elements shirtless, his skin felt warm and I couldn't stop myself from burrowing closer, seeking out more. His hold tightened around me and then we were back at the cabin and he was opening the door, walking in, and closing out the cold.

He didn't put me down. Instead he walked to the fire, stopped in front of it, and dropped to his knees again. He didn't speak, just held me in front of the dying embers with one arm while throwing another piece of wood on the fire.

My teeth wouldn't stop chattering. "G-god, I c-can't get w-warm," I said.

As soon as the words left my mouth, we were moving again. Hank carried me to the bed, sat me in the edge, pulled off the wet socks, tugged the sweater over my head, and grabbed the edge of the covers.

"In, Birdie."

I scrambled in and he threw them back over me, then stood there watching me. "Better?"

The cold felt like it had soaked right down to my marrow. Not as bad as when I'd gotten lost, but it wasn't pleasant either. My teeth were still chattering. "H-how are you not cold? You're n-not even wearing a s-shirt."

He shoved his fingers through his hair. "I'm used to the cold. I—shit, I'm not used to—" He cursed. "I should have put more clothes on you before I took you out there." He strode to the fire and threw more wood on then turned back to me, like that would make an instant difference.

I wasn't getting warmer. It was almost like I was making the bed colder, which I knew must be impossible, but that's exactly how it felt. I looked over at him, remembering how warm he'd felt and how cozy I'd been when I woke beside him the day before. I was too cold to care if it was inappropriate; I just wanted to be warm, and Hank was the source of some serious heat.

I shoved the covers back. "Get in…please."

His thick brows shot up. "You'll warm up soon. The fire just needs to—"

"P-please, Hank."

His huge body stilled, like a startled animal. Finally, after standing there, jaw working for what felt like forever, he moved to the bed. I watched as he undid his pants and shoved them down, so he was only wearing his boxers. My lower belly warmed instantly, and I swallowed hard.

"Move over," he said, a growl to his voice that lifted the hair on the back on my neck.

I did as he asked, and the bed dipped as he climbed in beside me. I had no shame at this point and rolled into his warmth immediately. I didn't know this man, we didn't know much about each other except for the little he'd told me, but I did know I could trust him. My initial fear had vanished sometime between him making me cocoa and being carried out in the snow to the outhouse in his strong, capable arms.

The big man holding himself unnaturally still beside me, arms crossed over his chest, clearly uncomfortable, was no threat to me. He was far from it. And I felt...safe.

I'd been on my own for a long time. Even when my mom had been alive I'd spent most of my time alone while she worked. There had been many occasions in my life when I'd felt unsafe or scared.

When was the last time someone held me? I couldn't remember.

I didn't have many friends. Well, you couldn't really call the people I spent time with friends so much as coworkers. I'd never had a best friend—we'd never stayed in one place long enough. We'd moved a lot when I was a kid, never put down roots.

I'd lost my mom eighteen months ago, and it turned out I was as restless a soul as she'd been. I was still living that life, sticking to myself, never staying in one place too long, and as nice as hugs and friends were, that was how I liked it.

That didn't mean I didn't want to feel close to someone, to feel a connection to another human being from time to time.

It had definitely been a while between *times*, though.

When I moved to Eaglewood six months ago, I'd busied myself with work, with the small garden at the house I rented, and my hobbies. I hadn't tried to meet anyone. I was also used to taking care of myself.

But I could admit that having Hank do that for me felt nice.

Really nice.

Heat radiated from his big body, and I was plastered to his side, but it wasn't enough. "Can you...w-will you p-put your arms around me?" I asked, teeth still chattering a little.

He said not one thing, just grunted and unfolded his

arms. I immediately took advantage and slid in closer. A shudder moved though me when I was finally surrounded with his intense warmth.

Slowly, the heat of his body soaked in, warming me in a way that was bone deep. My eyes got heavy and my limbs relaxed. I didn't have the strength to move away, my muscles feeling sluggish after being so tense from cold. My eyelids drifted shut.

I'd move soon.

3

BIRDIE

A LOUD, repetitive sound dragged me from my sleep, and I lay there for several seconds trying to work out what it was. A kind of whack/thump combo that made me jump every time I heard it. I sat up, shoved my hair off my face, and looked around the cabin.

I was alone.

Which meant the sound I heard was being made by Hank, since no one was getting on or off this mountain with the amount of snow currently outside. Pushing the covers back, I climbed out of bed and winced when my bare feet hit the worn rug by the bed. Even with the fire roaring, cold seeped through, plus my ankle was still smarting. I looked down. It was still quite swollen and bruised, but better than the day before.

My clothes were still on the rack above the fire, and since I had no clue how to work the thing and get it down, I limped to the dresser where Hank had gotten me socks last night and pulled open the top drawer. After a quick search, I discovered sweaters, pants, thermals, hats, and gloves. The cabin was well stocked.

There was no way I'd fit any of the pants, but I fished out a pair of thermal bottoms and tugged them on. They were way too big, so I bunched up the excess fabric, pulled my hair tie from my wrist, and secured it. Next, I dragged on a big green jumper over the shirt I'd already borrowed, followed by a pair of thick socks.

The sweater smelled like Hank mixed with that unmistakable scent of wool. Real wool, not that synthetic stuff, and was obviously hand knitted. It was well worn, had several spots that had been patched over the years, and was snuggly and warm. I pulled on a hat and headed for the door.

Yep, my ankle had definitely improved because I managed to slide both feet into my boots. I unhooked one of Hank's huge jackets by the door and tugged it on. It swamped me even more than the jumper.

I headed outside. It was snowing again. Maybe it hadn't stopped—I had no idea—though it was lighter than last night. I headed to the outhouse, quickly did my business, and then followed the *whack/thud* sound to the back of the cabin.

I found Hank.

He was chopping wood.

Oh my.

My mouth went dry.

He was wearing those outdoorsy-type pants that were cargo but also waterproof, and they fit him like a glove. He was also wearing a white thermal top with a blue and black checkered shirt over the top. Both had the sleeves rolled up revealing muscular, corded forearms. His longish hair was poking out the sides of a faded red woolen hat.

I watched as he picked up a chunk of wood, placed it on a large stump, then swung his axe. He brought it down hard with one mighty hit, rending the wood in two like it was a twig, not a massive branch. He bent forward, picked one piece up, and flung it onto the pile he'd already chopped.

I couldn't take my eyes off him. I mean I knew he was strong—he'd carried me five freaking miles—but still. The man amazed me.

He'd just flung the second piece when his head turned my way.

His massive frame froze for a split second, then his blue eyes moved over my body, taking in what I was wearing.

"I, ah...wasn't sure how to get the drying rack down to get my clothes," I said by way of explanation.

He didn't answer for a couple of beats, then said. "You should go inside, out of the cold."

I couldn't look away from him. If any man existed that was more masculine, more...God, manly, I would insist on seeing proof to believe it. Hank Smith was like nothing, no one, I'd ever seen before. Just looking at him made my belly feel funny and sent inappropriate thoughts shooting through my head.

He also aroused me to the point of insanity.

The man made me all hot and bothered. Which was crazy, especially when he could barely make himself touch me. He'd laid there last night, hands behind his head, while I wrapped myself around him like a python suffocating her next victim, trying to get warm. The man struggled to even make eye contact with me. He had been nothing but a perfect gentleman. He was no threat to me, not in any way. My freak-out when I first woke to find myself in his cabin had long gone.

Yes, despite the way he looked and where he lived, he was more of a gentleman than any man I'd met. The last guy I'd dated had been a wolf in sheep's clothing. He hid his true nature, only letting it show when he'd got what he wanted from me.

Hank hid nothing. I barely knew him, but I knew that. Right then I was as isolated as anyone could be, and I felt safer than I had in a very long time.

"Birdie?"

I jumped. God, I was still staring at him and he was waiting for me to do or say something. His brows lifted.

"Sorry, yes?" I felt my face heat.

"Get out of the cold," he said again, voice low and gruff. "I'll be in to make breakfast soon."

"Right." I forced myself to turn away and head back into the cabin. The least I could do was make him breakfast. He'd already cooked for me once, and going by what he'd told me, I doubted he'd had someone return the favor in a while.

Hank

I'd stayed outside for as long as I could. But the snow was falling heavier and I needed food. Birdie would, too. I walked toward the door to the cabin, and my gut tightened the same way it had last night while she'd lay almost on top of me, the lush softness of her curves pressing into me. A warm weight that had made me too hot, but craving more of her heat all at the same time.

I'd never experienced anything like it. I wasn't an idiot—I knew what I was feeling—I just had no clue what to do with it. A woman like Birdie would never want a man like me, and I wouldn't know how to please her even if I worked up the balls to do something about it. Humiliation washed over me. I should know this stuff. I should know how to act around a beautiful woman, how to exercise control over my body instead of having it respond like a hormonal teenager, but I didn't.

I wasn't like my brother. I hadn't had a lot of experience.

I'd only ever been with one woman. Roxanne lived in town, a good woman who made her money on her back and had offered herself as my nineteenth birthday present, free of charge. My grandfather had brought her out to the homestead after a visit to town for supplies.

He'd left her with me and gone hunting.

I remembered being excited, but feeling on some level it was wrong as well, that it wasn't what I really wanted. My body had grown achy and hard when she stripped in front of me, like it had last night when Birdie had lay beside me. Last night, though, there'd been no feeling of wrongness.

The episode with Roxanne had been fast. I'd rutted into her, let my body, my need to get off, control my actions. I'd felt disconnected from my mind the whole time. Then she'd screamed, and I'd felt her contracting around me, and I'd emptied myself, gasping and shaking like the inexperienced idiot I was.

She'd laughed afterward, teased me about my lack of stamina, and patted me on the cheek. *"Maybe next time you'll go a little longer, boy."*

A shudder moved through me and I shoved the humiliating memory from my mind, and pushed the door open.

The rich smell of bacon, beans, and eggs cooking hit me instantly.

Birdie stood at the fire, stirring a pot on the hot plate. She'd worked out how to get her clothes down and had changed into a pair of leggings and a fitting thermal that hugged all her curves. She was still wearing my socks, though, and the woolly hat. Her dark hair was loose, falling down her back.

She smiled at me. “I made breakfast.”

“We need to go easy on supplies. The snow hasn’t let up yet. We could be stuck up here for weeks.”

She bit her lip and glanced at the food she’d prepared. “Oh, of course. I just thought…I’m sorry, I guess I didn’t think.”

I felt like a giant asshole. “It’s fine,” I said. I didn’t know how to act around her, and that pissed me off. I shoved off my jacket and hat and hung them by the door.

She didn’t speak while she dished up what she’d cooked and handed me a plate. Her fingers brushed mine and a jolt shot up my arm again. *Jesus Christ.*

I dragged out a seat, sat my ass down, and started eating, trying to get my body under control. I should probably talk, make conversation. What the hell would I say?

I glanced over at her. She was in the chair across from me, her portion a lot smaller than mine, eating quietly. “Not used to company,” I muttered. I didn’t want her to feel bad, and obviously my gruff response to her cooking for me had done just that.

She glanced up and her big brown eyes caught mine. My gut tightened.

“When did you last have visitors?” she asked.

My gaze dropped to her full lips, then back up. “My brother visits when I’m down at the homestead.”

“That’s it? No one else?”

I shook my head and shoved in another mouthful. This was another reason I didn’t like talking: people wanted to know things, personal things about you. Assumed you were abnormal if you preferred your own company.

She lowered her knife and fork. “I don’t know how you do it. Don’t you get lonely?”

“No.”

We ate in silence after that, and then I went back to chopping wood. When that was done, I checked my traps. Rabbits were still fairly plentiful if you knew where to look. I could make rabbit stew tomorrow. I cleared and reset my traps—two wasn't bad, especially with this weather—and headed back to the cabin.

I'd stayed away all day, so I had no idea how Birdie had occupied herself. I was just counting down the days until I could get her off this mountain. I couldn't handle this restless, achy feeling in my gut for much longer. Didn't want to deal...shit, I didn't even want to think about the way she affected me.

I shoved the cabin door open and was hit with hot humid air and the smell of stew.

In the corner, where I kept my old tin tub, a sheet had been nailed up as a privacy screen.

"Hank?" Birdie called from behind it.

She had a camping lamp back there with her, which meant the white sheet might hide her, but her shadow was projected on it clearly. I could see the outline of the tub, as well as her shoulders, arms, and head. She was running a cloth along her arm.

She stilled. "Hank? Is that you?"

I quickly cleared my tight throat. "Yeah."

She started moving again, if I had to guess I'd say washing her shoulders.

"I hope you don't mind, but I desperately wanted a bath. I've already eaten. I heated up the stew from yesterday if you're hungry."

I grunted, unable to form actual words, and forced myself to take off my boots, coat, and hat, and dish up my dinner. I took my usual seat, then realized that wasn't such a great idea because I had an excellent view of what was going on behind that sheet.

I couldn't make myself move.

I couldn't goddamn eat.

I sat there and watched her. Every shadowed move behind that sheet, listening to the sound of the water splashing, moving with her. My head filled with images of her bare skin, wet and glistening. Of her running a cloth over her soft, full breasts, between her thighs...

My hand dropped to my stiff cock and I squeezed it, biting back a groan. I was about to get the hell out of there, go to the outhouse and do what I needed to do to make it go away, when she stood.

Her naked body was outlined perfectly, every lush curve. She turned slightly.

Fuck.

I could make out one of her nipples. It was jutting out, a hard, tight peak. My mouth watered.

Roxanne had had a beautiful body. She was slim and delicately curved. But it wasn't her I thought of when I stroked myself at night alone. The faceless woman in my head was soft, wide hips, rounded belly, bottom and breasts that overflowed my hands.

She was Birdie.

That faceless woman now had a face to go with that beautiful curvy body, and I knew it would be her I'd see from then on. Every time I closed my eyes and stroked my cock, it would be Birdie who was letting me do dirty, wicked things to her.

I needed to get up and leave, but the way her breasts swayed as she dried off and dressed had me mesmerized, glued to my goddamn seat, balls throbbing, cock harder than it had been in my life.

The sheet was pulled back and I dropped my eyes to my dinner, shoved a now cold forkful into my mouth, and started chewing. My face was hot, flushed, and that pissed me the hell off.

"Oh! You caught rabbits?" she said.

I sucked in a breath through my nose and lifted my eyes. She was in her own pants but was wearing one of my sweaters again. "Yeah."

She bit her lip and that caused another gut clench. "I've never eaten rabbit before."

I grunted, my eyes dropping to her breasts without my say-so.

"I hope you don't mind that I borrowed another sweater? They're just so warm and soft. They're hand knitted?"

"My mother knitted most of them for my dad."

She slid into the seat across from me. "She used to live up here?"

"She left when Beau and I were eight."

Her brown eyes widened. "She left you?"

I dipped my chin, not sure why I was sharing this stuff, but I was willing to do anything to stop the ache in my groin, and talking about my parents was sure to do that. "She left us and our dad. Didn't like it up here. Didn't like the solitude. Dad died a short time later. That's when our grandfather took over raising us."

Her hand slid across the table and her fingers curled around my wrist. "I'm so sorry."

I shrugged, but couldn't take my eyes off her hand on me. How small it was. How pale and smooth her skin was in contrast to mine.

My heart started to pound harder.

"Hank..."

I shot to my feet. "I need to check on something." I shoved on my boots, jacket, and hat and headed back out.

I spent the next two hours stacking wood behind the cabin, until the lights dimmed inside and I knew she was in bed. I waited another fifteen minutes then went back in. She was curled up in my bed, cheek resting in her hand.

I stripped down to my thermals and started across the floor to the makeshift bed I'd made by the fire.

"There's room in here," she said sleepily. "It seems silly for you to sleep down there when there's a perfectly good bed we can both fit in."

I started to shake my head, but she flicked the covers back. I glanced at her face. Her eyes were shut, and going by how relaxed her features looked, on the verge of falling asleep.

I started for the bed, intending to drag the covers back over her and go to my own bed, but when I got there I couldn't make myself walk away. Memories of her from the night before, how she felt beside me, her sweet curves pressed against my hard muscle, were so fresh in my mind. I craved that again, to feel her draped over me, the warmth of her body, the softness.

I slid in beside her before I fully thought about what I was doing.

Reaching over, I turned off the lamp beside the bed and stared up at the ceiling, watching light from the fire flick against the beams. I lay like that for what felt like forever. Birdie's breathing had grown deeper and even. She was asleep. She'd moved a few minutes ago onto her back, facing me, one hand on her belly, one on the pillow by her head. The blanket had dropped a little and I could see the swells of her breasts through her top. Her knee was cocked and all I could think about was that place between her thighs. The heat of it, her scent down there, how tight I imagined she'd grip the aching length of my cock.

Christ. It throbbed, resting hot against my stomach.

My breathing increased in speed, my heart pounding so hard it was all I could hear. I needed relief, and though I knew it was wrong in so many ways, I couldn't stop myself from sliding my hand inside my long johns and giving my dick a rough tug.

My back arched, and I couldn't stop from doing it again. I watched her sleep as I did it, her face, her breasts, her spread thighs. I imagined thrusting in and out of her, the feel of her soft curves pressed into me, her moans of pleasure.

I wasn't the incompetent asshole with little experience when I was in my head. In my head I knew how to please her, how to make her pussy grip me tight, how to make her wet, how to make her scream my name.

I stroked up to the head, twisting a little, then down to the base. The bed shook slightly, and Birdie's breasts swayed with the movement. I was lost to the sensation, to the images in my mind, the real-life vision of her beside me.

I gripped myself harder, stroked faster…

Something touched my arm. I jolted, my eyes shooting up to hers. They were wide, on me.

I started to yank my hand out of my long johns, but her grip tightened around my arm and she shook her head.

Her hand slid over my wrist, down to just above the waistband of my thermals. "Don't stop, Hank."

It should be impossible, but having her eyes on me made me even harder.

"Please," she said.

My fingers spasmed around my cock and I groaned. "No…I—"

"Please," she said again, moving closer.

Oh God. Another groan rumbled past my lips and there was no way I could stop from dragging my fist down my length and back after hearing her soft plea. My whole body shuddered harder than before with her watching me. My gaze stayed on her face as I stroked myself. Her eyes were still wide and she bit her lip, licking and sucking it. I was helpless to do anything else. Then she slid her hand lower, over mine, inside my long johns.

"Let me?" she rasped in a way that sent tingles across my scalp.

Another shudder moved through me, and without my say-so, my legs spread, giving her more room. My own hand gave way, slipping free to allow for hers.

Her soft, warm fingers wrapped around me and she gasped. "You're so hard, Hank."

Her words shot pleasure down my spine and my hips thrust up, forcing my cock deeper into her fist. Her fingers didn't reach all the way around, but her grip was firm and felt better than anything else I'd ever experienced in my life —until she slipped her other hand in as well and cupped my balls, massaging lightly.

That was all it took—a couple of tugs, her eyes on me— and a shout burst from my throat. I started coming in her hand. Pulsing so hard my spine torqued, my hips working frantically, each pulse of my cock shooting more come into my boxers until I collapsed back on the mattress, sweating and shaking.

Christ. A woman touched me, and I shot my load like a goddamn teenager. I'd come all over her hand like a fool. I waited for it, the laugh, the comment.

No, fuck that. I didn't want to hear it.

I shoved back the covers and climbed out of bed before she could say anything.

"Hank," she called after me.

I didn't turn around. I couldn't bear to see the look on her face. "That shouldn't have...that was a mistake." I quickly dressed. "Go back to sleep."

I heard her climbing out of bed, but I stomped outside before she reached me.

I spent most of the night shoveling snow away from the cabin. When I went back inside hours later, Birdie was asleep in the chair by the fire.

4

BIRDIE

HANK WAS AVOIDING ME. Not easy in this small cabin, which meant he spent most of his time outside. He'd also barely said two words to me since he walked out on me last night.

I'd just thrown a piece of wood on the fire when he walked in early afternoon.

"Just grabbing something to eat them I'm heading back out to check the traps," he muttered.

I watched him open a can of beans and start eating without even heating it. He was still in his jacket, hat, and boots. That's how desperate he was to get away from me.

"Hank..."

He put the can down—he'd only eaten half—and started for the door, ignoring me.

"Hank..."

He pulled the door open.

"What did I do wrong?" I said, the desperation in my voice so damn obvious.

He froze.

"Please tell me why you're so angry with me." I barely

knew this man, but I hated the thought of him being angry with me, that I'd somehow upset him.

He pushed the door shut, blocking out the cold wind, leaned against it, and pulled off his hat. "I'm not angry with you, Birdie."

He wouldn't meet my eyes and I could see his cheeks had darkened. "Well, what's going on? Why are you being like this?"

He cursed under his breath, his chest expanding with his rough inhale. "What I did...the way I acted..." He shook his head. "I'm...embarrassed."

What? I took a step closer. "Why? You have nothing to be embarrassed about."

"You caught me..." He cringed. "Doing...what I was. It wasn't right. I should never have done that beside you."

"I liked it," I said, voice nothing more than a whisper.

His brows lifted. "You did?"

I hugged myself. "Yes." This man—God, I'd never known anyone like him, never *seen* anyone like him. He was big and fierce and untamed, but there was a vulnerability under all of it that had my belly in knots, that made me want to know more about him.

That had me craving his touch like no one else.

"Watching you pleasure yourself." I took a shuddery breath. "I've never seen anything more beautiful in my life." I lifted my eyes lifted and locked them with his. "You're amazing, Hank."

His nostrils flared, but he said nothing. His eyes dropped to his boots and I could see his chest rise and fall rapidly. Finally, his eyes lifted back to mine and the way they burned made my knees weak. "What" —he cleared his throat— "what was amazing was having your hands on me."

Then he pulled the door open and walked out quickly, shutting it quietly behind him.

I stared at the door he'd just walked through and had to grab for the edge of the table as a wave of lust—God, need—like I'd never experienced in my life, washed through me. I hadn't cooled down since I'd felt the heavy, thick weight of his cock in my hand, since I'd watched him come. And as the time passed and I waited for him to return, it only worsened. My skin seemed to get tighter, my breasts fuller, and despite the snow again falling outside, I was hot, flushed with need.

I ached, and I found myself squeezing my thighs together as I distractedly chopped carrots for the rabbit stew I'd made. I'd never used rabbit meat before, but I'd made stew, so I hoped it tasted good. It smelled good, not that I was hungry. Not for food anyway.

It was probably more than two hours before I heard the sound of boots crunching through the snow, before I heard the door rattle and Hank walked back in.

He didn't say anything as he took off his boots, coat, and hat. But when he turned to me and his gaze hit mine, the need curled tighter in my belly so hard and fast, oxygen was shoved from my lungs.

"Smells good," he said, voice low and rumbly.

I felt that, too. I squeezed my thighs together tighter. "You have..." I walked toward him, stopping a foot away, and even though he'd just come in from the cold I could feel the heat radiating off his big body. "You've got snow in your beard." I reached up, because I wanted to touch him, and brushed it away. I took another step closer. "And in your hair." I did the same to the hair at his neck where the hat hadn't reached.

His nostrils flared, and I watched in awe as the giant in

front of me shuddered, a full body quake that had him sucking in a harsh breath. The top of my head only hit mid chest, so when he took a jerky step toward me, his body colliding with mine, I stumbled back.

His arm shot out and he hooked me around the waist, yanking me into the muscular wall of his body. I gasped when I felt the hard length of his cock against my belly.

"Birdie," he rasped out past windblown lips.

I tilted my head back, staring into the blazing heat of his eyes. "Tell me what you need, Hank," I whispered.

The muscle at the side of his jaw jumped. "I can't stop thinking about your hands on me."

"M-me either," I said, my breathy choppy and shallow.

His large hand came up to the side of my face, thick, long fingers gently skimming across my cheek. "You're so beautiful."

I curled my fingers around his forearms, not wanting him to let me go. "So are you."

He frowned, even as his cheeks colored. "I...I don't know what to do."

My pulse raced faster, out of control. "You've never been with a woman?"

His cheeks got darker. "Only once, a long time ago."

Oh God. I searched my mind for the right words. "What do you think about when you're on your own, when you're stroking yourself?"

"You," he said, so rough it was like fine sandpaper abrading my skin, but in an intensely good way. "I never knew her face, not until I lifted you out of the snow, stripped you down, and put you in my bed." His hot gaze moved over me. "Everything else, everything...it was you."

Somehow, I managed to speak past my tight throat. "What do you do to me?"

"So many things, Birdie. So many dirty things."

I pressed against him as he stepped closer. My back met the rough-sawn wall and I lifted a hand, curling my fingers around the side of his thick neck and brushed my thumb over his beard. "I'm here now."

He growled.

I shivered and licked my suddenly dry lips. "You don't have to fantasize anymore, Hank."

Another animalistic sound vibrated through his chest, making my nipples tingle, then one of his huge hands landed on my butt and he hauled me effortlessly up. I instantly wrapped my legs around his waist and my arms around his neck.

"I want to kiss you," he said.

"Then do it," I whispered, pulse racing.

He licked his lips, and after a moment's hesitation, brought his mouth down on mine. He kissed me in a way that was rough and out of control, unschooled. His beard was soft and prickly all at once, and tickled my chin. There was no finesse, no holding back. It was wet and hard and as untamed as the man himself. It was the hottest kiss I'd ever experienced.

His tongue tangled with mine, his growls shooting straight to the aching need between my thighs, and I couldn't help but rub against him, seeking relief, needing more of him.

His hips slammed forward, and he ground into me. "Birdie," he said between rough breaths and rougher kisses, a desperation in his voice that had me soaking through my panties.

My fingers slid into his hair at the nape of his neck and I held tighter as his powerful body continued to thrust against mine. The hard, unforgiving length of his cock ground into me through our clothes, hitting my clit just right. I dropped a hand, shoving it under his shirt, and my fingers came into contact with the hot, smooth skin of his back. The muscles bunched under my fingers. I thrust my hand down the back of his pants, digging my nails into his firm-muscled ass cheek.

He tore his mouth from mine, panic crossing his expression, as well as a lust so deep and wild my pussy clamped tight and I started coming.

He gasped. "I can't stop"—he shook his head—"I have to..."

He grunted, then shoved his face against my throat and groaned low and long, shuddering, hips jerking against me as he came as well.

"I'm sorry," he gasped against my overheated skin. "Christ, I'm pathetic...I'm..."

I cupped his face, encouraging him to lift his head. "Why would you say that? Hank, you did nothing wrong." I shook my head. "You did everything right. You made me come so hard. God, I'm still feeling it." I bit my lip as my pussy pulsed again.

"You did?" he asked, voice pure grit.

I shivered. "Yes." And moaned when he pressed into me and another wave of pleasure shot through me.

I knew he could see it on my face that I was telling the truth when he sucked in a sharp breath through his nose and his gaze dropped to my chest. I watched as his hand lifted to my breast and cupped it. His thumb swiped over my nipple and I shivered again.

"That felt good?" he asked.

"Yes."

"Could you come again?"

I nodded, my hips rolling against him.

"Will you..." he gritted out. "Will you show me what to do?"

I swallowed, trying to get moisture back in my mouth. "Yes."

His eyes dropped lower. "Can you...if I put my mouth on you...if I lick your pussy..." He lifted his eyes to me again. "Can you come that way?"

I nodded again, words no longer an option. Then I watched in awe as the huge mountain man in front of me dropped to his knees. He looked up at me as he slowly, cautiously, gripped the top of my thermal pants and started dragging them down my legs. Usually I was self-conscious about my abundant thighs, but with the way Hank was looking at me, the only thing I felt was beautiful.

I stepped out of my pants, and then his fingers were sliding under the sides of my underwear. He looked up at me again, and I gave him a small nod. "Do whatever you want, the things you've fantasized about."

When his eyes dropped back to my cotton-covered pussy, my thigh muscles started to quiver.

He started to tug my underwear down, and when they reached my ankles and I stepped out, his monster chest shuddered.

"Spread wider for me. Please, I-I need to see you," he rasped.

I did as he asked and his whole body convulsed, like an electrical current had fired through him.

"Birdie," he groaned on a ragged whisper. "You're... Christ...do you have any idea how many times I've fantasized about this?" His hands at my ankles started sliding up.

I shook my head.

"About this body, this...pussy." He gritted his teeth, like

he was struggling with his control, like he was trying desperately to hold himself back.

I didn't want him to hold himself back. I threaded my fingers through his hair and tugged gently.

He groaned and pressed his nose to my mound. "Your scent—fuck." His head tipped back, and his eyes locked on mine again. "You're so perfect."

My heart was racing at his words, with the anticipation of having his mouth on me, from the way he looked at me. He took one of my legs and lifted it over his shoulder.

A second later he pressed his hot mouth against my slick pussy lips and growled.

The vibration of it felt amazing, then his tongue darted out, moving over me tentatively, testing, tasting.

That's when his control snapped.

5

HANK

OH FUCK.

The words spun around my head over and over again. This was happening. I couldn't hold back. Her scent, her taste. Birdie had wrapped herself around me so tight, had crawled so deep, I couldn't think straight.

All I knew was that I wanted to please her. I wanted to make her come against my tongue, hear her scream in pleasure. I didn't know if what I was doing would do that, and I hated that I didn't so much, that I was so damn inexperienced. Beau would know. I'd walked in on him like this with a woman, her thighs on his shoulders. The look on her face said she loved it. God, I hoped Birdie did, too.

My cock pulsed, hard as iron again, as I licked up her juices and she squirmed against me. I dragged my tongue through her slit up to her clit. I knew from Beau that was one of the ways to get a woman to come, and going by the way Birdie tugged on my hair harder and ground her pussy against my mouth, I was doing something right.

Her moans grew louder, so I lifted her other leg, cupped her soft ass, and ate her like the starving man I was.

"Hank," she cried out. "Oh God, please, please don't stop. I'm going to..."

No goddamn way would I stop.

I wanted to feel it, I wanted to feel the way her body reacted to what I was doing. She said I could do what I'd fantasized about, and I wanted inside her in a big way. So, I pressed the tip of my finger to her tight little opening and started to slide it inside.

She gave my hair another tug. "Yes...yes, push it deeper."

Knowing that I was doing this right, that I was making her feel good—nothing compared to it. I felt taller, stronger, more of a man than I had in my whole life. I continued to lick and suck her perfect little clit while I slid my finger in and out of her. She was hot and wet and tight. I wanted it to be my cock. God, so bad.

I was pulsing hard and my balls were drawn up tight. I shoved my free hand down the front of my pants, my shoulders holding Birdie up, and tugged on my cock. I fucked her with my finger while I fucked into my fist.

I felt her clamp down on me at the same time her scream filled the cabin. I kept at her, licking her stiff clit and thrusting my finger inside her as she ground against me, trembling and moaning. The sounds she made alone would have been enough to send me over the edge, but with everything else, the feel of her, the taste, the scent...knowing it was me that was pleasing her, making her feel this good...

I blew the hell up, grunting and growling as I shot my load into my boxers for the second time.

Birdie went lax, so I carefully lowered her legs, lifted her in my arms, and carried her to my bed. She lay there staring up at me, bare from the waist down, the sexiest, most beautiful, perfect woman I had ever seen in my life.

"Climb into bed with me, Hank."

Her voice was husky from her screams. The sound of that and the sight of her relaxed and satisfied made my chest expand with pride.

A knot curled in my gut as I stripped off. I used my boxers to clean myself off, and climbed in beside her. She rolled into me immediately, the soft heat of her body soaking into mine.

I decided to ask for what I wanted again, like she told me to. "I want you naked." I wanted to feel all of her against all of me.

She immediately pulled her shirt off, followed by her bra. My hands had minds of their own and I cupped her breasts, massaging, weighing them, loving the way they overflowed my hold. I did this for a while, indulging myself, running my hands over her body. Finally, I trailed my fingers lower, and her thighs spread for me instantly.

My chest puffed up again at the way she bit her lip and arched when I cupped her pussy, sliding my index finger through her slit.

"I want to make you come again, Birdie. Can I?" I surprised myself by asking. It felt so good to make her feel good—Christ, addictive—that I wanted that feeling, that high again.

She nodded, eyes wide, chest rising and falling faster.

I played with her, my hand between her thighs, watching her every reaction, following her huskily spoken orders when she gave them. *Faster, deeper, harder.* Until she screamed again. Then I did it again, this time not needing instruction, and once more, until she passed out.

I spent the night watching her sleep and making sure the fire burned hot enough that covers weren't necessary. I didn't want to cover her beautiful body. I wanted to memorize every dip and valley, every dimple and freckle.

I also prayed.

For the snow to keep falling.

"What's your favorite color?" Birdie asked, trudging along beside me.

Her ankle was a lot better, good enough to trek with me to check the closest traps and look out for logs I could cut up for firewood. My food stocks were good, but I wanted enough that going down the mountain wasn't something we had to do because we were forced to. The snow had stopped two days ago. The powers that be had ignored my prayers, not that I believed in all that. They hadn't listened when I begged for Him to bring my mother back or for my grandfather to get better. I had hoped, though, that I would get a little more time with Birdie. It was wrong, but I hadn't even suggested taking her home. Another day and we could get down without too much trouble. But I wasn't ready for that, to let her go.

I knew I couldn't keep her forever, but the urge to stay there, away from the real world, her world, was getting harder and harder to ignore.

I looked down at her. She looked cute in one of my woolen hats, her dark hair down and wavy around her shoulders and back.

"Don't have one," I said, answering her question, one of many.

She frowned. "Really?"

I dipped my chin.

She tapped her chin. "Okay, favorite type of cake?"

"Chocolate."

She smiled. "Mine, too. Can you bake?"

I shook my head, trying to ignore the way her smile made my heart race. “My grandmother used to make me one every year for my birthday.”

Her smile got wider and I had to look away.

“Winter or summer?” she asked next.

“Winter.”

She snorted. “Why doesn’t that surprise me? Well, me and the cold really shouldn’t mix. Or mountains…or snow.” She grinned up at me again.

My gut clenched even tighter. “You’re doing all right,” I said.

“Well, it feels good to be out of the cabin. I was going a little stir-crazy staring at the same four walls.”

I grunted, not wanting to think about what it meant, but I couldn’t stop the thoughts spinning around my mind. I knew firsthand that this life wasn’t for everyone, and as much as I wanted to keep her, Birdie was no different. She’d soon grow tired of the solitude, the loneliness. She’d long for her old life, and she’d ask me to take her home. She had a life waiting for her, one that didn’t involve me…or my *four walls*.

She tucked her hair behind her ear. “My mom and I moved around a lot. We have travelling souls, you see. Well, that’s what she used to say. I think it was more she couldn’t make rent., so we skipped out.” She chuckled softly. “We always stuck to warmer places. I stupidly decided to try the mountains. They are beautiful, though. But I guess I’ll be moving on soon.” Her gaze slid to me then darted away. “I wouldn’t want to break tradition and stay in one place too long.”

The idea of her leaving, of me never seeing her again…

“Oh look! Is that one of your traps?” She was pointing to one of the snares I’d made to catch small prey.

"Yeah." It was empty. I didn't care, I was still processing the fact that soon she'd be gone.

She turned to me. "I know you said you don't get lonely, but don't you just...I don't know, crave human contact sometimes?"

Her cheeks were flushed and when she said that they got darker. We'd had quite a lot of human contact over the last few days. I'd been learning every way I could make her come, how many times I could make her come before she passed out. We hadn't done much more than that. I knew she wanted to do things to me, too, but I hadn't really given her the chance. She'd said I had nothing to be embarrassed about, but it was there in the back of my mind, hovering, messing with me. That same humiliation I'd felt all those years ago.

I didn't want to disappoint her.

And since I was obsessed with pleasuring her, I was more than satisfied.

Yes, I wanted her.

So much so I was in a constant state of arousal, but getting my fix, hearing her screams, was my drug.

"Not really," I said, answering her question about getting lonely.

It wasn't a lie, or it hadn't been before I met Birdie. Now I wasn't sure how I would survive not being able to touch her, talk to her, sleep beside her. I didn't tell her that, though. There was no use. Saying those things was pointless.

She chuckled, and it sounded forced. "I really don't know how you do it." She started walking again, a little ahead, which meant I couldn't see her face, but there had been a note to her voice that gave me pause, something I had no hope of understanding.

We checked several more traps. She watched me reset

them and even carried a rabbit, but she was quiet. I didn't like it. Something I'd said had upset her, but I couldn't for the life of me work out what that was.

I wanted to make her smile again.

"Can I show you something?" I said, surprising myself.

She glanced back at me. "Sure."

"Your ankle will hold up?"

She nodded, curiosity clear in her eyes.

I led her to the familiar path. It was still under snow, but it was packed and not that deep. I used to come up here all the time, but these days just once or twice a year. The track was narrow and rocky in places, and when Birdie grabbed for my hand to keep her balance I kept hold of it, not wanting to let her go. I didn't think I'd held anyone's hand since I was eight years old. Holding Birdie's, her smaller one wrapped in mine, gave me more pleasure than should be possible for such a simple act. That point of connection commanded all my attention. Everything about it was etched in my brain.

It took only fifteen minutes to reach the clearing.

Birdie came up beside me when I came to a stop, and I watched her draw in a deep breath, taking it in. "What is this place?"

"Over there." I carried on walking, leading her to my favorite spot. It was just across the clearing, and when I stopped again, I turned to her, wanting to see her reaction, hoping that she loved it as much as me. I watched her cheeks flush with pleasure, and her eyes go wide with wonder.

"Hank," she whispered. "This is...it's beautiful."

I'd always thought so. "My grandfather used to say you could see the whole world from up here."

She stared out at the view and her smile got brighter,

sucking the oxygen right out of my lungs. "I think he was right."

I couldn't take my eyes off her. "He used to have a cabin up here when my dad was a kid. It wasn't much, but they loved it. One real bad winter, the roof caved in, and a lot of it was destroyed. Getting building material this far up was tough, so they decided to build the new hunting cabin lower down the mountain, somewhere less exposed." I stared out across the mountain range. "I still come here, though. Beau, too."

"I can see why," she said.

I turned to her, swallowing the lump growing in my throat. "I feel closer to them when I'm up here."

She tilted her head back and looked up at me. "Your dad and your grandfather?"

I rubbed the back of my neck, suddenly feeling uncomfortable. "Yeah."

She gave my hand a squeeze. "How did they die? You were still young when your father passed?"

I hadn't talked about this for a long time, but I wanted to share something with Birdie, something that would let her know she meant something to me. "My grandfather got cancer. I took care of him until the end. He refused to leave the mountain."

Her eyes softened. "That must have been extremely hard for you."

"The least I could do after everything he did for us. Would've done anything for him." I shrugged. There was never any other choice, not for me. "My father, an accident. Broke his leg while out hunting. He died from the cold before my grandfather could find him."

I watched her pale, and I knew she was remembering how close she'd come to the same fate. I shoved the same thought from my mind. I couldn't bear to think about it, what I would have found if I hadn't got there when I did.

"I'm so sorry," she said.

God, she was beautiful. "Loss, it's just...it's part of life."

"Yes, but that doesn't mean it hurts any less, or that those losses don't leave scars." A gentle smile curved her lips. "Thank you for showing me this place, for sharing how important it is to you. It really is breathtaking up here."

She was breathtaking. I wanted to kiss her.

"Birdie..."

A yowl echoed across the clearing and I spun around.

A short distance away, a mountain lion, still a cub, rolled in the snow in a panic, hissing and yowling.

"She's caught on something." There was no way I could leave it like that.

Birdie grabbed my arm.

"I'm going to try and free it. Stay back," I said.

Where there was a cub, there was a mama, and there was no way I wanted Birdie anywhere near either of them. I got closer and could see the cub's leg was caught in an old chain. It snarled and lashed out, but I managed to hold it down. It was scared and making a lot of noise. The more it thrashed, the more tangled it got.

I was trying to free the animal, and look out for Birdie at the same time. I knew its mother wouldn't be far away, and when I heard the growl a short distance from us a few minutes later, it lifted the hair on the back of my neck. I saw movement at my side. Birdie had come closer.

"Don't move," I said to her. "Stay completely still."

I kept eye contact with the mountain lion, staring her down as I blindly worked on the chain tangled around her cub's leg. Crouching down was not a good position to be in, but I didn't have much choice. "I know you're angry, mama, but I'm not hurting your baby," I said, voice low, not taking my eyes off her once.

The chain loosened. One last tug and the chain came free. The cub sprang up and ran straight to its mother. She didn't move, but continued to hold my eyes, full of aggression. I needed to appear as large as possible, so I slowly rose to my full height.

"Go now," I said, low and firm.

Finally, she spun around and they both ran off.

Birdie instantly collided with my back, her hands tangling in my jacket. "Oh my God. I've never been more terrified in my life."

"They're gone. She won't come back," I said. "I'm not going to let anything hurt you, Birdie."

I felt her nod against my back. "I know that. I knew you'd keep me safe."

My chest expanded to damn near twice the size. I loved that she knew that, that she felt safe with me. She continued to cling to me, and I liked that, too. I didn't want her scared, but I liked being the man she turned to when she was, the man she knew would protect her.

I reached back, took her hand, and pulled her around to my side. "We better head back."

She nodded and started walking, but stayed close the whole way.

I loved that, too.

When we got back to the cabin, Birdie started heating up leftovers from the night before, and I half-filled the tub to have a wash. I couldn't fit my bulk in there, unlike Birdie who could get right in. The sheet was still up, even though we didn't really need it now. I'd seen all of her, every stunning inch, but I left it there for her in case she wanted privacy while she washed.

I stripped off and stood in the tub, soaping up quickly, and washed off. I could hear Birdie humming as she worked. The sound was sweet and soft, and the more I listened the harder I got. I felt closer to her after today, and it was messing with me, making me want her even more than I had before, which I thought was impossible. By the time I finished, my cock was so hard it stood up against my stomach.

My breathing grew choppy as I thought about Birdie stroking me that first night. I'd never felt anything so good.

I quickly climbed out. I'd been rubbing myself off while I ate her pussy every night, but last night I'd humped the fucking mattress until I blew, with my face buried between her thighs. I dried off, willing my cock to calm down.

The sheet slid back, and Birdie poked her head around the side. "You nearly ready for dinner?" Her voice trailed off and her eyes moved over me, my shoulders, my arms, my stomach...lower.

Her mouth dropped open.

"I'll just..." I grabbed for my pants.

"No," she said, shaking her head. "No, leave them off."

The way she was looking at me...I swallowed. Hard. "Birdie..." Her name rumbled past my lips, a plea, a warning, I had no idea what it was. I just knew I had to somehow control myself. Be a goddamn man and not act like some untried teenager. I could do that, couldn't I?

Christ. After today, I couldn't take another second without her touching me.

She moved in closer and took my hand, leading me out by the fire. It was dark outside and the only sound was the crackling wood and wind rattling the windows...and my unsteady breaths.

How did she do this to me? One touch and I'd do anything she asked me to. Anything.

My cock pulsed and my knees almost buckled. I looked down. My cock was dark, veins bulging along its length, pre-come glistening at the head, and she hadn't even touched me yet.

She rested a hand on my chest and dragged it down over my abs. They tightened under her fingers. "You're like an ancient warrior," she said. "So big and strong. Capable, protective." Her eyes lifted to mine. "I've never felt as safe as I do with you. Never. Today, what you did, faced with that mountain lion, I've never seen anything like that in my life."

I wanted to ask what had made her feel unsafe in her life, who had made her feel that way, but her hand slid lower, and instead of asking her those things, I looked at her and groaned.

She moved in close, so the front of her body was pressed against mine, trapping my stiff cock between our bodies. "You've made me feel good every night, Hank. You've made me come so many times and not taken anything for yourself."

"I wanted to," I choked out. "Making you feel good, I can't get enough."

"I want to make you feel good, too," she said softly.

My chest was pumping with my rapid breaths. "Please," I said, my control slipping more and more by the second.

It was all I could manage. I wanted that. I wanted whatever she wanted to give me. I'd take anything as long as she was touching me.

"Sit on the chair, Hank."

I did as she asked without question, lowering my ass to the chair, stomach clenching, thighs quivering. I'd hang from the goddamn rafters if it meant having her hands on me. Her hands went to my knees and she pushed them wide as she lowered to her knees in front of me.

Her big brown eyes came back to mine. “Has anyone ever taken you in their mouth? Sucked you?”

I shook my head. *Oh God*. I wanted that. I wanted that more than anything.

6

BIRDIE

I STARED AT HANK, huge body held unnaturally still, eyes filled with so much longing it tore me to shreds just looking at him. He looked so wild and untamed. A giant sitting there waiting for what I'd do next. His skin was golden despite it being winter. His chest hair was thicker over his pecs, a dusting over his abs. He was sitting with his solid thighs spread, his heavy balls and achingly hard cock on full display.

He was a sight I would never—could never—forget.

Knowing that he wanted me that much, that he would do anything I asked in that moment, was empowering. Made me feel beautiful. The last guy I'd dated had shaken my confidence terribly with his backhanded compliments and at times outright negative remarks. I'd always liked my body, my curves, but in the short time I'd gone out with the jerk, he'd managed to inflict damage. He'd made me feel differently about myself. Hank was helping me get that back, and all he had to do was look at me.

I slid my fingers around the base of his hard cock and gave it a squeeze.

He groaned and thrust up into my fist. "Birdie," he said, voice more growl than anything else.

"You ready, Hank?" Just looking at him like this had my thighs slick and my clit desperate for attention.

"Yes," he gritted out.

I dragged my hand up his length, my mouth watering as I leaned in and dragged my tongue across the head, lapping the pre-come from the tip. Hank bucked and barked out a rough sound.

I slid my hand down, then back to the tip, and looked up at him. "You taste so good, Hank."

His hands rested on his thighs and his fingers curled into fists.

On the next downward stroke, I took the head of his cock into my mouth and sucked nice and hard. The chair legs thumped against the floor from the way his body jolted. I couldn't take all of him into my mouth, so I continued to stroke and squeeze and twist the base as I sucked him as deep as I could manage. My other hand was resting on his thigh and I grabbed for his, wrapping my fingers around his wrist and bringing his hand to the back of my head.

His fingers threaded through my hair instantly.

"Birdie..." he groaned. "Christ, sweetheart..." His hips lifted a little, forcing himself deeper. "I'm sorry..."

I took him deep again, without him thrusting up this time, to show him I was okay, that whatever he did was okay.

The broken gasp that filled the cabin when I cupped his balls and lightly squeezed was the sexiest thing I'd ever heard in my life.

"Sweetheart...oh God, your mouth...I've never..." He groaned again like he was in pain, like the pleasure was too much. "Christ, Birdie."

I sucked him harder, faster. He throbbed in my mouth,

and actually seemed to grow thicker. I swallowed down more of his salty pre-come and I knew he was just about there.

His thighs bunched on either side of me. "Feels so good, I can't stop it...I'm gonna come...I'm..."

He tried to pull away, but I sucked harder, letting him know what I wanted.

His fingers immediately tightened in my hair, fisted, and his hips jerked forward. My eyes started watering, but I took it, giving him what he needed, swallowing rapidly when he shot down my throat.

He grunted, a sound that morphed into a long growl, before he moaned my name over and over again, chanting it like he couldn't stop. I kept sucking and licking him while he shook beneath me, until he fell back into the seat, spent.

I released him with a pop and looked up at him, letting the happiness I felt over being the one that gave that to him show on my face.

He cupped my cheek, his thumb sliding across my puffy, tingling lips. "Jesus, Birdie, I..." He shook his head. "That was incredible."

I stood, and he grabbed my hand.

"Are you wet?" he asked.

I drew in a shaky breath. "Yes."

He tugged me closer, then gripped the sides of my pants and tugged them and my underwear down my legs. I opened my mouth to say he didn't need to return the favor, but the words turned to a startled squeal when Hank threw me over his spread knees. My bare ass was in the air and I gasped when his hand slid between my thighs.

His fingers slid back and forth between my drenched pussy lips, and with a grunt of approval, he pushed one inside me, nice and deep. I bit down on the thigh supporting my head and thrust back into his hand. "Is this one of your fantasies?" I gasped against his thigh.

He dragged the finger out then shoved it back in, adding a second. "Yes," he growled.

My scream was muffled by his muscled thigh. I spread wider for him, welcoming his thrusting fingers.

"Had a lot of time to imagine what I'd do to you when I finally found you, Birdie. Naked, over my knee while I played with you, making you wriggle and squirm and come all over my fingers was one of my favorites."

Oh God. He went deep, so deep, fucking me like that. His other hand slid under me and he cupped my breast, squeezing, teasing my nipple.

"Love these," he said. "These big soft tits. Love your ass, and your hips and your cute rounded belly. Fucking perfect, Birdie."

His blunt words made my head spin, and turned me on even more than I already was. His thumb was resting against my behind, lightly pressed against my hole and it felt good, so damn good.

I tried to push back, but I was being held down over his knee, completely at his mercy. His work-rough palm and thick fingers worked between my thighs, and I loved it. I loved that it was me who he was showing this side of himself to.

He thrust in hard, and I jolted and bit deeper into his flesh. He worked me over and over, teasing my G-spot, driving me to the edge. And when he next pushed inside, he stayed deep, thrusting shallow rapid thrusts that, combined with his thumb pressing harder against my ass and the way he tormented my nipple, had me coming with enough force to knock me unconscious. I screamed, loud enough to scare away any animals in hearing distance.

Hank gently removed his hands from between my thighs and under me, and then they were moving over me, massaging, caressing. I lay there unable to move for the longest time. Not wanting to.

Finally, I lifted my head and caught sight of my teeth marks on his skin. "Oh God, Hank, I'm so sorry."

He lifted me like a limp rag doll, which was exactly how I felt. "I like them," he said, all deep and gruff, then carried me to the bed.

He was hard again, painfully so.

Hank came down on top of me, his mouth attacking mine with a hunger that set me alight right along with him. I gripped his shoulders, the bulging muscles flexing under my hands, and spread my legs for him automatically—which put the head of his cock *right there.*

I moaned.

His hips jerked forward at my needy sound, and he slid in about an inch, stretching me.

He tore his mouth from mine. "I'm sorry." Strain lined his face. He was breathing heavily, and his arms shook. "I shouldn't have done that. I—"

I dug my heels in when I thought he might pull out. "God, don't stop. Fuck me, Hank, please. Fuck me."

He hovered above me, eyes burning into mine, and I watched a change come over him. His stomach muscles, his thighs, God, every muscle in his body tightened—a reminder of his immense strength, of how badly I wanted him to let that loose on me, to give me everything. He was hanging on to his control by the thinnest of threads. Watching as it washed from his face, as animal need took over, sent anticipation spiking through me.

A growl exploded past his lips, and his hips snapped

forward. His cock thrust into me, filling me completely. I cried out as a string of curses flew from his mouth.

He held himself still above me, staring down at me, breath hissing through his teeth. "I've only done this once before. If I do something wrong, something you don't like, tell me, sweetheart. Please, tell me."

It was impossible to form an answer when my body was still adjusting to him, to his size, so deep inside me. All I could do was cling to him tighter.

On a groan, he pulled out and slid back in.

We both groaned.

Then he really started moving.

His big body covered mine, rolling, driving into me. His grunts and growls filled my head, and I felt his muscles bunching beneath my hands as he thrust into me over and over again.

He looked down on me, jaw tight, teeth clenched, the tendons in his neck bulging under his skin, and I moaned his name.

"Christ, wrapped around me so tight. So tight, sweetheart," he said, voice as rough as gravel.

I dug my heel into his firm ass and twisted my hips, grinding into his next thrust.

"Oh God, oh fuck." He squeezed his eyes shut tight. "You can't do that. You can't move on me like that. I won't last, and I want this to last."

His face was flushed, his expression hiding nothing. The man was sweet and fierce all at once. "I'm nearly there already, Hank," I said. "You're perfect. This is perfect."

His eyes opened, and his hot gaze dropped to my chest, to my swaying breasts. "Look at you," he bit out. "Goddammit, Birdie, my fantasy girl brought to life. Don't want this to end. Never want this to end."

His whole body went solid and I knew he was holding back, waiting for me to come first. He didn't have to wait long. With the next thrust and grind of his hips, I screamed, my pussy clenching around his iron-hard length repeatedly as it drove into me without mercy.

"I can feel it, can feel you...so good," he gritted out. Hank wrapped one of his brawny arms under my hips and hauled them off the mattress, pulling me down on his cock as he thrust up, filling me over and over again, filling the air with more of his sexy grunts and growls. All I could do was hang on and take it, take each exquisite, brutal thrust of his powerful body.

I watched in awe as his head flew back and he groaned loud enough to rattle the windows, making me shudder with every pulse of his cock as he shot hot and hard inside me.

He collapsed on top of me then quickly rolled to the side, taking me with him, and he hung on tight.

I absorbed his warmth and let my eyes drift shut. I was asleep in minutes.

I woke in the middle of the night. Hank was on his side curled into my back, heavy arm over my waist, snoring softly. I even liked his snoring. I liked knowing he was there, that I wasn't alone.

I liked the way he looked at me, the way he made me feel like the loveliest woman he'd ever seen, like even if we were in a room full of beautiful, perfect women, it would only be me that he'd see.

I liked it all, everything that was Hank. In fact, I was pretty sure *like* wasn't a strong enough word for what I felt for Hank Smith, not by a long shot.

God, what we'd done—I had never experienced anything like that in my life. I was slick between my legs, traces of Hank, of the way he'd taken me, still there. I'd never had unprotected sex in my life. But I hadn't even thought about it last night. Thankfully, I was on the pill. And I couldn't regret it. I would never regret one moment of my time with Hank.

But I knew it was time to go, that there would be people worried about me. They probably thought I was dead. I didn't want to leave, not this cabin, not Hank. But Hank liked his own company. Soon he'd want his solitude back. He didn't want anyone else in his life.

I'd never quite felt like I fitted in anywhere. When I was with Hank, though, it felt right. Being there with him felt right.

I needed to go back down the mountain, to my little rental house, before I got even more attached to him than I already was. I needed to go back to the real world, a world that was lonely, and would now be even lonelier because there'd be no Hank in it.

I squeezed my eyes shut, but it was no use. The first tear fell, followed by the second.

Somehow, I'd fallen in love with Hank Smith, and tomorrow I had to tell him to take me home.

HANK WALKED IN WITH AN ARMFUL OF FIREWOOD AND DUMPED it in the wood bin by the fire.

I watched him, the way he moved, the sounds he made, the intense look in his eyes. Always intense.

Always searching.

When he looked at me sometimes, I thought he was trying to get inside my head, that he wanted to read my thoughts. I was obviously imagining it. The fact that he hadn't asked to know more, to learn more about me and my life, said it all really. He didn't want to know more because there was no point. I hated the way that stung.

Hank wasn't some player, some jerk using me to get his rocks off. He was a good man, a man used to being on his own. And he liked it that way. At least he'd been honest.

I'd just finished making the bed, so I moved toward him, stopping on the other side of the table. "It looks good outside. Clear."

His back was to me and he stilled like he often did, in that unnatural way, like if he was still enough no one would notice him. Did he know he did that, that he froze when he was out of his comfort zone?

He grunted in response.

"It hasn't snowed in three days," I said, pointing out the obvious, trying to get him to talk to me. There was a reason he hadn't taken me home as soon as it cleared. Would he admit it? The real reason he hadn't taken me home yet?

He still wasn't looking at me. "Yeah," he said.

I forced myself to say the words I'd been dreading all night. "I was wondering if maybe...if the trails were clear...if it was time to go home?"

He turned to me, his eyes not meeting mine. "Your ankle..." He rubbed the back of his neck. "You think it's strong enough?"

I took him in, his posture, the way the muscle at the side of his jaw jumped, the way his fingers curled and uncurled at his sides.

Hank knew as well as I did that my ankle was fine. It had been fine for days. I'd even gone to check traps with him. Was this...

My eyes shot up to his. He still wasn't looking at me.

He didn't want me to go.

This was his way of asking me if I felt the same, if I wanted to stay up there, with him, for longer. My heart started to race. God, I did, so much, more than anything in the world. But prolonging this would only prolong the pain. The end.

I had to get back to the real world and stop living in this fantasy one.

"Hank," I called, and his eyes finally landed on mine. I felt my lower lip tremble, but I made myself say what needed to be said. "Yes, it's...it's strong enough."

He flinched, and I felt it, like someone reaching into my chest and squeezing until I couldn't breathe.

Finally, he dipped his chin. "We'll leave first thing in the morning."

He didn't say much after that. Neither of us did. What was there to say? I knew once we reached the bottom of this mountain, once he delivered me home, I wouldn't see him again. I also knew I'd regret it for the rest of my life if I didn't spend one more earth-shattering night with him. If I didn't tell him, show him, how much he meant to me.

I was still trying to work up the courage to say it, to ask him if he'd give me that, as it grew late. We'd eaten, I'd cleaned up, and it was nearing the time we usually went to bed.

Tonight, things weren't the same, though. Hank seemed edgy, distracted, and my heart had been racing since I'd decided to tell him I needed to go home.

The air in the cabin felt thick, electric. The tension was so dense my limbs felt weak. He wouldn't make the first move, though, not tonight, not after I asked to leave.

I turned to him. "Hank."

He lifted his head and when his eyes locked with mine,

the oxygen was knocked from my lungs. "Yeah?" he rumbled, voice thick, pure gravel.

"Tonight's our last night, and I...I want..."

He stood, resting his closed fists on the tabletop. "What do you want, Birdie?"

"I want for us to—"

The door banged open and a fur-covered monster stomped in.

My hand flew to my chest and I stumbled back. Hank was around the table, catching me around the waist before I could fall, and held me there.

"Jesus Christ, Beau," Hank gritted out.

Beau?

The monster shoved back a fur hood. "Surprise," he said, then his eyes slid to me. "Though it turns out the surprise is all mine." His eyes lifted to Hank. "Who do we have here?"

Beau was almost the spitting image of Hank. Maybe not quite as built. Still big, but not Hank big, though I doubted many were. They were about the same height. Beau's beard was trimmed, not as long, and his hair was a little shorter.

But the main difference was the smile on his face. I'd never seen Hank smile, not like the one curving Beau's lips.

And you never will.

"Why are you here?" Hank said instead of answering.

Beau frowned. "You know why I'm here. You were due back three days ago."

Hank cursed. "Lost track of time."

"I can see why," Beau said.

Since Hank wasn't offering up any information, Beau's eyes slid to me. "I'm Hank's brother, Beau." He slid off his gloves and held out a hand to shake.

"Birdie," I said, taking it.

“I take it I’m interrupting?” He grinned, but I could tell by the way his eyes slid back to his brother that he was full of questions. He was far more shocked at finding me there with his brother than he was letting on.

“Hank rescued me. I got separated from my group. I was lost and then Hank showed up. I would have frozen to death if it wasn’t for him.”

Beau’s eyebrows shot up. “Birdie Winters?”

“How did you know?”

“They think you’re dead.” He cursed. “Since the snow’s finally let up, they’d planned a search party. They’re heading up tomorrow...to bring down a body.”

Oh God. I felt ill.

Beau shook his head. “What the hell were you thinking?” he said to Hank. “Why didn’t you bring her down two days ago when the tracks started to clear?” He pulled something from his pocket.

“She hurt her ankle. Couldn’t move her,” Hank said.

Beau gave me a once-over. “She’s not favoring it now. Seems all right to me.”

I felt my face heat.

Beau’s gaze came back to my face, then it shot back to Hank and he grinned again.

“Don’t say one fucking word,” Hank growled.

“Wasn’t going to.” Beau held something up. “You’re lucky I have this.” He glanced at me. “Satellite phone. I’ll call, let them know you’re safe and well and coming back...” His brows lifted, waiting for an answer.

“Tomorrow,” Hank said.

I listened as Beau made the call, then he helped himself to leftover dinner and plonked down in one of the chairs around the table.

Hank was quiet, surly, sitting opposite him. I was in the only armchair in the room, by the fire.

Beau looked at Hank and smirked. "If you weren't so damn stubborn and bought a goddamn phone I wouldn't have had to come all the way up here. I'm the one that should be pissed, not you."

"I'm not pissed."

Beau snorted. "You look pissed from where I'm sitting."

Hank growled.

Beau laughed.

I sat there, fascinated, watching the exchange. They were so alike in appearance, but that was as far as it went.

"I can see why you'd be annoyed, of course..."

"Beau," Hank said, warning clear in his voice.

"You must have known I'd show up here when you didn't arrive home?"

Hanks jaw tightened. "Like I said, I lost track of time."

"I'll bet," Beau said, then his eyes slid to me.

Hank shot to his feet, grabbed his brother by the back of his sweater and shoved him toward the door. "A word. Outside."

Beau winked at me and let his brother push him out the door. "We'll be right back."

7

HANK

GODDAMN BEAU.

How could I have forgotten my brother? We always let the other know how long we'd be up here for. We took each other's backs. Our grandfather had drummed this into us as kids. We always had a return date and if one of us didn't show, the other went looking.

We'd never had to go looking, which was why I didn't even think about it.

"Tonight's our last night, and I...I want..."

What did Birdie want? I had a feeling—a strong feeling—I knew exactly what she wanted from me, and Christ, I wanted to give it to her again more than anything in the world. Over and over. Now I might never get to be with her again like that, and it was my own damned fault.

My earth had moved on its axis last night. Making love to Birdie had been life altering. My feelings for her went far beyond lust—they had before I knew what it was to slide deep inside her, but now? Christ, I wanted to give her a lot more than that, more than the physical, I wanted to give her everything.

"You can quit shoving," Beau said. "We're out of earshot."

I gave him one last push for the hell of it. "Why did you have to show up tonight?"

Beau actually looked sorry. "I thought you'd fallen on your giant head and needed me to save your ass. Brother, this is not my fault. You really need to get a sat phone."

He was right, of course. This was my own fault. Beau was only making sure I was all right. I cursed.

Beau stared at me, brows low. "What's going on here?"

My face heated. I hated it. We'd talked about women before, but it was always Beau doing the talking and me doing the listening. That's the way it had been our whole lives, and not just when it came to women.

"You're sleeping with her?" Beau asked.

"No, I'm—" I cut myself off, not able to lie.

Beau winced. "Shit, Hank, I'm sorry, man. I messed up your night."

I shoved my hand through my hair. "I don't even know if that was going to happen again tonight. I mean, we've done it—" I cut myself off again, feeling uncomfortable, something I never had around my brother.

Beau grinned again. Bastard. "She's a beautiful woman." His head tilted to the side. "You like her, don't you? A lot."

There was no point lying, Beau could read me, just like I could him. "Yeah."

"You going to see her again?"

I shook my head. "What's the point? Birdie likes to move around. She likes new places, new people. She said herself she couldn't live like this."

Beau thumped me on the shoulder. "Shit, man, I'm sorry."

My brother got it, he understood. He might work on a ranch

during the summer, but that was only to save enough money to finish building his house. I'd inherited our grandfather's place, and we'd split the land, but my brother needed his own home.

Beau had left for a while, tried life off the mountain, and had quickly worked out it wasn't for him. So, yeah, he got it. If we ever decided to settle down, get married, and have kids, we had to find a woman who could handle this life, or we'd end up like our father.

"I hardly know her. We've spent a week and a half up here together, that's all. She'll go back to her life, and I'll carry on with mine. I'm just..." I shrugged. "I feel something for her and I wanted her to be—I wanted..." I cursed again. Taking about this was so goddamn hard.

"You wanted to spend one last night with her." Beau finished for me.

I dipped my chin.

"For what it's worth, the way she was looking at you in there, she wanted the same thing."

I thought he might be right.

But there was nothing for it. I'd have to go back to life without her.

I'd have to go back to settling for fantasies.

WE'D BEEN TREKKING FOR A FEW HOURS, STOPPING REGULARLY so Birdie could rest. Beau took the lead and I took the rear, making sure one of us could catch her if she tripped or fell.

We'd left first thing this morning, after a shit night sleep. I'd slept on the chair and Beau on the floor. I wanted to lie beside Birdie one more night, but I didn't trust myself not to touch her.

She seemed fine. Had been chatting the whole time. Glad to be going home. I didn't want Birdie to be unhappy, but seeing just how happy she was, it stung.

I'd kept quiet as Beau asked her all the questions I hadn't asked her, questions I'd desperately wanted to ask.

"So you're an only child?" Beau asked. "How old were you when your father left?"

"Yep, it was just me. He left when I was a baby. Mom raised me all on her own, but she died when I was eighteen."

"I'm sorry," Beau said. "Do you have any other family?"

She shook her head.

We'd both lost our parents, only Beau and I had been lucky enough to have our grandfather. She'd had no one.

"Who watched out for you?" I asked, speaking for the first time in more than an hour. But I had to know. The idea of Birdie being all on her own, with no one to make sure she was safe and had what she needed, was more than I could stand.

She glanced at me over her shoulder.

"Eyes ahead," I said.

"Right, sorry," she muttered.

She wasn't used to this type of terrain, and as much as I wanted her eyes on me, I wanted her to not sprain her ankle again more.

"And no one," she added, eyes trained forward. "There wasn't anyone to watch out for me, but then I was used to looking after myself. My mom had to work; she had all my life. I was used to being alone."

I hated that so much it burned like a ball of fire in my belly.

"I guess you'll have a big welcome home party to look

forward to when you get back," Beau said. "Your friends will want to celebrate that you're okay."

She was silent a beat. "I don't really have many...um, well, I kind of just—" She cleared her throat. "I move around a lot, and I work, but other than that I don't really socialize much."

She didn't have many friends? I assumed she picked up new friends wherever she went.

"I don't really like crowds. Lots of people make me nervous. I like quiet, solitude. I guess it's my own fault. I don't go out much or try to meet people. Well, going on a hike in the mountains with a group of strangers had been my first attempt in a long time, and look how that turned out."

Beau glanced back at me and I could see exactly what he was thinking.

What the hell were you talking about last night? She'd be perfect for this life, asshole.

Beau hadn't spent a week with her, though. He didn't know about her travelling soul. And there was solitude and there was living on a mountain away from all civilization with a man who avoided people like a contagious disease. From what Birdie had said while we were at my cabin, she understood the difference, and the way I lived my life wasn't for her.

An hour later we were coming over the ridge to the homestead.

"See just over there," Beau was saying. "You can see the roof."

"Oh, yes, I see it."

My gut tightened. For some ridiculous reason, I wanted her to see my place. I wanted her to like it...no, love it.

Idiot.

It wasn't like she'd see the home my grandfather built my grandmother, the place where my father then Beau and I had been raised, and fall in love with it.

Fall in love with me.

But, God, I wanted that. So damn much.

Birdie

I walked into Hank's house and did a slow turn. It was gorgeous.

A lot of rustic wooden furniture, but all the solid pieces had the smooth edges of time and use. These pieces had been made, used, and loved by the Smith family. More than one generation. The house was two levels. A spacious living area with a huge open fire made of stone was at one end. There were two couches, one worn, sage green velvet and the other, a faded chintz fabric. Both had quilts across the backs that were obviously handmade by someone who had a talent for sewing. The kitchen was off that and it was a decent size. There was also a large family dining table that could seat ten people. The door that was open off the kitchen, from what I could see, led to what looked like a mudroom. I assumed the back door was out there as well and possibly a bathroom.

I'd imagined myself living in places like this when I was a kid. Even without the fire lit, the place exuded warmth.

This was a home.

The kind of place you put down roots and never walked away from.

"You want to see upstairs?" Hank asked.

I spun toward him. I hadn't even noticed he'd come in from outside, too busy marveling over his beautiful home. I looked beyond him. "Where's Beau?"

"He carried on to his place. It's only a couple of miles that way." He pointed toward one of the living room windows, out to the forest beyond. "Eaglewood's a two-hour drive on a shitty road. Better if we take you back in the morning." Hank pushed his hands in his pockets and tilted his head to the stairs. "You want to see the rest?" he asked again.

We were alone. For the whole night. "I'd love to."

He headed for the stairs. "I've got electric here now. Put up a wind turbine last summer. So, got an electric stove, lights, water heater."

"It's amazing. Your home...Hank, it's beautiful."

"My pops built it for my grandmother after they married."

I smiled. "He must have loved her very much."

Hank's eyes were locked on me. "He worshiped the ground she walked on."

His words were low and guttural, and I felt them all the way down to my toes. Then he headed up the stairs and I followed. He led me into a bedroom. There were big windows on two sides and a double bed with an amazing bedframe made of logs that still had their natural shape but had been sanded and varnished. I walked to the window and took in the spectacular view. It was late afternoon and the sun was dropping low in the sky. In the distance beyond a group of pines I could see another roof peaking from between them.

"Is that Beau's house?"

Hank moved up beside me and dipped his chin. "We've been building it for the last few years."

"I bet it's as lovely as this house," I said.

His head swiveled to me on his thick neck and his eyes were bright when he said, "It's pretty close."

I dragged in a deep breath at the look on his face, the way he was looking at me, the way it affected me, and turned to look back out the window. "The view from here, it's magical. Is that all your land?"

"Mine and Beau's."

God, this place was stunning, quiet, peaceful. "I can see why you love it here so much."

"Yeah?"

I nodded. "You have a beautiful home, a lifestyle that a lot of people would kill for." I smiled at him. "You know what you want and where you belong, Hank. Not everyone gets that in their life. I envy you." I'd never felt that, not once. Even when my mom was alive. With the apartments we lived in, the constant moving, I never once had that sense of home, of security, of belonging.

He stared at me for several long seconds, the air getting thicker the longer we stood there.

"Is this your room?" I said into the tense silence.

He shook his head. "Spare room. Mine's down at the end of the hall. There's another one next door and a bathroom beside that. I got a septic tank here, so the shower, bath, and toilet's inside."

"A shower?" I'd kill for a hot shower.

"Water's already on, so you can go ahead and use it whenever you want."

He showed me the rest of the house. He didn't go into his room, just shoved the door open and said, "My room." His bed was huge, with the same amazing rustic log frame and gorgeous quilts. There were windows on two sides in there as well, a large dresser beside the door, and several faded rag rugs on the floor.

We headed back downstairs, and I grabbed my meager

possessions. "I might just grab that shower now, if that's okay?"

"Of course. You can use anything of mine if you want clean clothes. Just grab something out of my drawers." He moved to the fire and set about lighting it, his back to me.

I stood at the foot of the stairs, my heart beating faster, my body hot and aching from just being in the same room as him, and forced myself to ask, "Which room should I put my bag in?"

He went still, in that way he always did, but didn't turn to look at me. "Choice is yours, Birdie."

The choice was mine.

I rushed upstairs. I'd been determined to spend another night with him, and I wanted to still, but as much as my body and my heart were screaming at me to take my bag to Hank's room, my head was shouting her opposition just as loud.

I was in love with him—there was no denying it. If I slept with him, let him make love to me, I didn't know if I would ever recover.

I quickly showered, and on my way back, since I was still undecided about what I should do, I dropped my bag inside the door of the spare room closest to the stairs. When I came down, the fire was blazing, and Hank had made an omelet for supper. While we ate, I asked him questions about his life growing up there.

I had no idea what time it was. We'd been talking a long time, and it was dark outside. A wave of exhaustion washed over me. The fire had warmed the large house easily, and after the walk there today, I was feeling it.

I didn't want to go to sleep, though—not yet. This was our last night together.

Hank went upstairs to use the bathroom. He was up

there a little while, and when he came back down he seemed different, quieter.

He picked up the plates. "I'm calling it a night. We'll leave first thing," he said, then he stomped up the stairs and vanished.

I stared after him, my heart racing again.

He'd obviously seen my bag in the spare room. He was disappointed. I sat there for several minutes, trying to decide what to do.

In the end, my heart—my body—was screaming louder than my head.

If I didn't go to him tonight, I'd regret it for the rest of my life.

8

BIRDIE

I WAS positive I hit every creaky board as I made my way up the stairs. There was no way he didn't know I was coming. Well, he thought I was coming up to sleep in the spare room.

I wasn't.

Nerves twisted tighter as I walked past the first bedroom. I had no idea why I was anxious. It wasn't like we hadn't had sex before. But this was different, wasn't it? Tonight, I wanted to give myself to him, show him how I felt, take that next step...even though that step led nowhere. Because not experiencing that with him one more time was unthinkable.

What if he'd changed his mind? What if he turned me away?

It was a risk I was willing to take. Since my mom died, I hadn't taken a lot of those. My life had been in constant upheaval for a lot of years and I'd wanted the opposite of that. But instead, I'd taken the easy route, the road I was familiar with, and I'd clung to it.

I didn't want to be that girl tonight.

The door was slightly ajar, and I gave it a little push. His room was dark but there was an orange glow from a small fire on the right. I hadn't noticed it when Hank showed me around. It hadn't been going. It was down to embers, left to burn out.

"You need something, Birdie?"

I spun around to the huge bed on the other side of the room. It was too dark to see Hank clearly, but the moonlight provided enough light that I could see the looming form of his impressive body sitting on the side of his bed. His elbows were on his knees and his head was in his hands. Those beautiful, big, rough hands.

I knew instantly that he'd lit that fire for me. He'd wanted me there with him tonight and when I put my bag in the spare room, he'd let it go out.

"Yes," I whispered. "I need something."

I watched him drop his hands and twist to me, silent a beat. "You still hungry?"

"No," I said softly, shakily.

"There are more blankets in the hall cupboard if you're cold."

"No, I'm not cold." I took a step closer.

More silence. He'd gone still.

I watched his wide chest shudder, and heard the sound of his rough exhale. "What do you want, Birdie?"

I was halfway to him. He still hadn't moved, but I knew he was watching me. The way the moonlight filtered in meant that I was under its spotlight and he was in shadow, but I knew his eyes hadn't left me once. I kept coming until I was right in front of him, only a few inches from his spread thighs. Reaching out, I cupped his jaw, his beard prickling my palm, and slid my thumb over the warm skin of his cheek just below his eye.

He took another shuddering breath.

"Birdie..." he rasped.

"I want you, Hank, before tomorrow comes and this ends."

His hands shot out and gripped my waist, fingers digging in, and he groaned as he tugged me forward, filling the space between his splayed thighs with my body. His head dropped forward, resting against my chest, and those strong hands slid up and down my sides.

I threaded my fingers through his hair and gently tilted his head back, so I could see his face. "Do you want me?"

His fingers dug deeper, pulling me in closer. "Yes. Christ, so much."

He was only wearing his boxers. I was still dressed, so I tugged off my sweater and proceeded to strip under Hank's hooded gaze. When I was down to my panties, he grabbed my hands and held them behind my back.

"Let me just look at you," he said, shaking his head. "Fuck, Birdie. I dreamed of you, sweetheart, before I found you that day. I dreamed of you, but I never thought...I never thought..." He leaned in and pressed his mouth to belly, cutting himself off.

Oh God.

I kept my fingers firmly in his hair as he dragged his mouth over my bare skin up to my breast, drawing a nipple into his mouth, teasing me until the hard peaks were dark and tight and so sensitive I thought I might actually come that way. But then he moved lower until his lips teased the top of my underwear.

One of his hands left my waist and cupped my pussy, middle finger pressing deeper, giving much-needed pressure to my aching clit, and making me moan.

"So wet, sweetheart. Soaked."

"Yes," I said and shamelessly spread my legs wider for more of his touch.

Shoving my panties aside, he pushed a finger inside me, and then his mouth was there, sucking my clit through the damp fabric. I cried out and used my grip on his hair to hold him there, never wanting him to stop. That long finger of his had no trouble finding and working me deep inside, and when he added a second and pushed even deeper, a gush of wetness left me. Going by his growl, he'd felt it, felt what he did to me, how much I wanted him, how close I was to coming around his thrusting fingers.

"Oh God...I'm going to..." His fingers vanished, and I was lifted, spun, and planted in his bed. I cried out, frustrated at being deprived of his touch, of the orgasm that was only seconds away.

Hank covered me, shoving my legs wide. I gasped at the feel of his massive erection, and ground up against him, lost to the pulsing need I had for him.

"When you come, it's going to be around my cock again, not my fingers, Birdie."

"Yes," was all I could manage to say.

The sound of tearing fabric filled the air as he tore my underwear from my body. I reached down and shoved his boxers over his ass. One of his hands moved between us and he shoved them down at the front, freeing his beautiful cock.

"Please," I said on a moan. "Please, Hank. God, I need you."

He made a pained gasping sound and buried his face against the side of my neck. "I...fuck," he bit out. "I don't think I'll ever stop wanting you."

My head was still spinning from his words when I felt the head of his cock nudging against me, dragging through my slit, through my wetness, then pressing against my opening. I spread wider for him, accommodating his massive body, and cried out when he started pushing inside, filling me. I clawed at his back, sucking and biting at his shoulder as he stretched me wider, wanting more, wanting to feel him thrusting into me with all his immense power.

"You feel so good, sweetheart, so perfect and warm and tight," he said through gritted teeth. "So wet for me. That's all for me, isn't it, beautiful? You love the feel of me inside you?"

Did he even need to ask? I turned my head, my mouth to his ear. "I've never wanted anyone the way I want you."

I felt a shudder move through his frame, then his hips snapped forward and he filled me to the root, giving me all of him. I screamed and dropped my hands to his ass, digging in my nails. Wanting more. Wanting everything. He lifted his head, and his mouth came down on mine, his tongue thrusting in time with the thrust of his hips. He slammed into me over and over in a way that was all about animal need, about listening to his body and what I did to him.

I felt my orgasm rushing me, and knew it was going to blow me apart. I had no control over my thrashing limbs, my nails scoring his skin, or over the sounds I made.

"Don't stop, never stop," I cried as I started tightening, spasming around him, crying out as it hit, and fired through me. My toes curled, and I was only half aware of Hank lifting to his elbows above me. I held nothing back, absorbed it all, released everything, gave it all to him. If this was our last time together, I refused to hold one damn thing back from him.

When the last waves of pleasure washed over me, forcing helpless moans past my lips, I opened my eyes.

Hank was hovering over me, his gaze moving over my face, intense, dark, hooded. Fierce.

He was still hard, his thrusts slower but powerful. "You're so beautiful, Birdie. Watching you like this, Christ… I'll never forget a second. Never."

He started moving faster, more intense, but he didn't bury his face against my neck. He stayed where he was, eyes locked on mine. I saw it when he was about to come—could see the way his features tightened, the way his mouth flattened—and I was right there with him again, another orgasm building inside me hard and fast.

His body started trembling and I held him tighter.

"Birdie…" God, the sound that left him was close to a sob as his thrusts got wilder, the rhythm unmeasured. "Only you," he said, then he grunted out my name over and over, his cock pulsing inside me, filling me with everything he had.

HANK

Birdie lay curled into my front, her face buried against my chest, each exhale tickling my chest. I'd woken up hard, but with her warm breath on me, her smooth soft curves, her small hands holding me, I was getting harder by the second.

Her face as she came apart under me flashed through my mind. I'd never forget it, never. Thinking about letting her go, taking her home today, physically hurt. But I couldn't hold her here, no matter how much I wanted to. I couldn't keep her trapped in the mountains and expect her to be happy.

How could I be enough for her?

I couldn't; I knew that much. My dad, Beau, and me, we

hadn't been enough for my mom. I'd watched her fade over the years, lose the sparkle, the joy in her eyes, until she finally couldn't take another minute stuck out here and walked away, never looking back.

I couldn't, wouldn't do that to Birdie, no matter how much I wanted her, how much I loved her...

I love her.

Birdie moaned softly, and tingles shot down my spine. Her hands gripped me tighter, her arms sliding around my belly, and she nuzzled her face against my chest. I thought she might still be asleep, but then she tilted her head back and smiled up at me. Her eyes were sleepy and hooded, hair wild around her face and shoulders.

"Hey," she said, voice still husky and sexy as hell from sleep.

Christ, she was beautiful. My gut clenched, and my cock pulsed against her soft belly. "Hey."

She pressed a kiss to my throat, no hesitation, then gently nudged my shoulder with her hand. I rolled to my back and she immediately climbed on top of me. Her smile turned to a grin, and my heart stuttered behind my ribs then burst into action, hard and thumping as I looked up at her.

"I want you, Hank. You okay with that?" she said, eyes not hiding one ounce of what she was feeling in that moment, how true her words were.

I lifted a hand and curled it around the side of her head, my fingers burrowing in her warm hair. "God, yes." I pulled her down and kissed her, deep and wet, filled with everything she was making me feel as well.

She ground her wet pussy against my stomach and I growled, my hips thrusting up, seeking her out all on their own. She didn't break the kiss, but reached behind her, gripped my erection, lifted her lovely round ass, positioned me, and stank down, talking all of me inside her in one downward stroke.

I groaned, my hips snapping up again at the exquisite feel of her wrapped around me, so hot and wet and perfect. But I kept my eyes on Birdie, watching as she rose up, the way her mouth dropped open as I filled her, the way her cheeks grew more flushed with every passing second.

Her hands slid up my chest, nails digging in, then she rolled her hips, squeezing around me at the same time. I barked out a curse, my hands going to her hips to hang on.

She bit her lower lip and did it again. "God, Hank, y-you're so deep."

My fingers sunk into her flesh hard enough to leave bruises, holding her tighter. Sweat beaded my forehead and it was taking everything in me not to roll her to her back and pound into her over and over again. "Fuck me, Birdie. Please, sweetheart, I need you to fuck me."

Goosebumps lifted over her skin then she started moving—really moving. Lifting up and grinding down, working her hips against mine in a way that had the ability to make me insane. The sounds of our lovemaking filled the room: panted breaths, her gasps and moans, my deep grunts, wet flesh slapping wet flesh.

Her breasts bounced and swayed, and I gripped one in my hand, shuddering at the way she overflowed my fingers, at the feel of her tight nipple against my palm.

She moaned desperately.

Then I felt it, felt her clutching my cock over and over again. Her scream echoed around the room as she came for me—and I lost it. Curling my arm around her waist, I flipped her to her back and went with my instincts. I hitched one knee high, so she was spread wider, so I went deeper, and pounded into her with frenzied thrusts that jarred her whole body and had her tightening more, screaming all over again.

My own orgasm nailed me, and I slammed forward, filling her as deep as I could go. I roared like the animal I was in that moment, filling her with my come, grunting with every pulse of my cock.

My body trembled so hard the bed shook. I pressed hot kisses over her cheeks, her forehead, her lips. "So perfect, sweetheart, so damn perfect. What will I do without you?" I gripped her tighter, shoved my face against her throat, and kissed the racing pulse there. "What am I going to do?"

9

BIRDIE

HIS WORDS SWAM around my head. What was he saying? Or was it just something he'd said in the heat of the moment?

I was trying to figure out how to reply when a door slammed. "Yo!" Beau's voice echoed up from downstairs.

Hank stilled a split second then lifted his head. His eyes didn't meet mine. "We better get up. We've got a long drive ahead of us."

My fingers flexed, pressing into the dense muscle of his back, and I watched his eyes slide shut. He leaned in, pressed a kiss to my mouth, then rolled away.

I wanted to pull him back and never let him go.

FROM HANK'S HOME, WE COULD TRAVEL BY TRUCK TO TOWN. There wasn't really a road, more like a track, but my aching thigh muscles were thankful for it. I wasn't sure I could walk another mile. I was sandwiched between Hank and Beau, since he needed supplies from town, and I found myself leaning into Hank, soaking in every bit of him I could before I had to say goodbye.

Beau chatted the whole way. Hank stayed quiet.

The two-hour drive flew by, far quicker than I would have liked. We dropped Beau off in the center of the small town to get what he needed, and my heart raced as Hank looked down at me.

"Where's your place, Birdie?"

I gave him directions and we drove there in silence. Finally, he pulled up outside the small cottage I rented and turned off his truck. We climbed out and he walked me to my door.

I found my key in my backpack and let myself in. Hank followed me inside and I watched as he took in my small home. I sewed and did a lot of arts and crafts to fill in my weekends, since they were usually spent on my own, and Hank was absorbing it all.

My couch was covered in cushions and had a patchwork quilt over the back. "You made those?" Hank asked.

"Yes." I hated how husky my voice sounded. The sadness I was feeling was coming through loud and clear.

"They're nice," he said. "My grandmother used to sew."

"I assumed the quilts must have been hers when I saw them. She was talented."

He turned from my couch, gaze coming to me. "She loved it. Often filled her days in her sewing room." He shrugged. "She loved the life; it suited her. My grandfather was a lucky man to find that."

"You don't think you ever will?" I asked, my heart in my throat.

His Adam's apple slid up and down his thick neck as he swallowed. "It's a hard, lonely life. I think..." His jaw tightened. "I think I'd be asking too much of any woman to live out there with me."

I would, in a heartbeat.

The thought shot through my mind, sucking the oxygen from my lungs. That wasn't me, though, was it? I didn't stay in one place.

I didn't know how.

He rubbed the back of his neck. "Good thing I prefer to be on my own, I guess."

And there it was.

Even if I decided to try and live in one place, to put down roots, it wouldn't be with Hank. He didn't want me, not in a permanent way, and, God, that hurt. I guess it was my own damn fault for falling for him, for letting my feelings run away with me when I knew there were reasons, good reasons, we couldn't work.

"Yes...good thing," I said, and it came out as a whisper.

I took a step back, suddenly needing distance from him, before I said or did something to humiliate myself. Like throw myself at his feet, wrap my arms around his legs, and beg him to take me back with him. "Right, well, I better call my boss and tell him I'm back. I need to get groceries and..." My words were cut short by the lump lodged in my throat.

Hank's eyes hadn't left me, not once. He dipped his chin. "I better go find Beau."

"Of course." I forced a smile. "Thank you, Hank, for everything. You saved my life and I'll never forget that."

His whole body tightened—like he was holding himself back? That was probably wishful thinking. But then he'd made no secret that he enjoyed my company, in his bed, anyway. The attraction between us was one thing that was real, unlike my delusions of us together as anything more.

Suddenly, he was moving toward me, but he didn't

scoop me up and kiss me silly or carry me to my bed and take me one last time. He leaned in and kissed my forehead.

I squeezed my eyes shut, and worked hard not to let the tears welling in my eyes spill over.

"Goodbye, Birdie."

"Bye, Hank."

Then he turned away and walked out the door.

His truck started a few minutes later and I walked to the window and watched him drive away.

Tomorrow, life would go back to the way it was before—no cabin in the mountains, no sitting by an open fire, no warm body beside me every night...

No Hank.

HANK

I gripped my steering wheel and forced myself to keep driving away, away from her.

"Good thing I prefer to be on my own, I guess."

My own words ricocheted around my skull.

It was a lie.

I thought I did, before Birdie. Before I knew what it was to have her in my life. God, I'd only said it so she wouldn't feel sorry for me, so she wouldn't pity me. I'd seen the look in her eyes.

Pity for the recluse living alone on his mountain.

What else could it be?

I saw Beau standing on the side of the road, grocery bags by his feet, and a woman at his side, talking to him.

My brother's arm shot out when he saw me, so I didn't miss him. I pulled over and he put his bags in the back, climbed in, and we headed off.

"Thank God you came when you did, Nadine Cooper was starting to get handsy." Beau said, then sat back.

I said nothing. My head was full of Birdie, of how wrong it felt driving away from her. How much I didn't want to leave her in that small house all alone.

"Yo, Hank?"

I glanced at my brother.

His brows lifted. "I called your name like eight times."

I shrugged.

I felt Beau's eyes on me and knew he was building up to say something. It didn't take long.

"Did you make a date to see her again?"

I shook my head.

"Why the hell not?"

"What would be the point?" I said.

"You slept with her again?" Beau asked.

"That's none of your damned business."

"You slept with her again," he said, this time it wasn't a question. "Brother, you've had opportunity to be with women before, and you chose not to. Birdie was different, though. I could see it the minute I walked into your cabin. You wanted her, no doubt, but it was more. You feel something for her."

"Leave it, Beau. I'm not talking about this."

"Mom hurt you, she hurt all of us, when she left and never looked back. Don't let her do it again, Hank. Don't give her that power. Don't assume every woman you meet is like her."

"Please, Mom, don't leave." I ran after her.

She stopped when I grabbed her hand, and looked down at me. "I have to, Hank. Being here...it's killing me," she said then pulled away from me, climbed in the truck, and drove away.

I turned to my dad. How could he let her leave us? How could he let her leave me? My dad turned and walked away, but I didn't miss the tears in his eyes.

I realized in that moment there was nothing he could have done to make her stay.

She just didn't want us anymore.

I shoved the memory to the back of my mind where it belonged. "I said I'm not talking about this."

"You're making a mistake," Beau said.

Was I? All I knew was having Birdie for close to two weeks and walking away was like tearing out my heart and leaving it at her feet. I wouldn't survive if she gave me more, made me hope for more, then left.

Neither one of us spoke for the rest of the drive. I dropped Beau at his place and carried on to mine.

Once I got home, everything would be okay. Everything would go back to normal, to life before Birdie.

But when I walked inside and looked around, I saw her everywhere. In my living room, sitting by the fire, walking up the stairs. She'd only been there for one night, but the mark she'd left behind was profound.

When I climbed into bed that night, I could smell her on my sheets, could remember the way she'd felt pressed against me...the way she looked straddling me this morning, riding me.

The way she looked when she came apart for me.

I stared at the ceiling.

What the hell was I going to do?

10

HANK

I HEARD Beau's truck before I saw it. It was as old as dirt, and after he finished building his house, he planned on buying a new one. None of these things were happening fast enough as far as Beau was concerned, so I did everything I could to help him.

I finished nailing down the sheet of roof iron that had come loose, slid my hammer in my belt, and climbed down the ladder.

Beau climbed out of his truck and tossed something my way.

I caught it. The nails I'd wanted. "Thanks."

Beau reached back into his truck and came out with a bag in one hand and a plate in the other.

He grinned. "Beer and" —he lifted the plate higher— "cake."

I smirked. "One of your admirers?"

Beau started toward me. "Nope."

"Where did it come from?" I asked as we headed to the seats on the porch.

"Birdie," Beau said casually.

I stumbled up the step, then spun to face him. "Birdie? You saw her?"

Beau followed me up the stairs, took a seat, pulled a beer from the bag, and took his sweet goddamn time answering me.

He twisted off the cap, took a sip, and sat back. "Yep."

Yep?

Asshole.

I hadn't seen her in two goddamn weeks and I was slowly losing my mind. "You want to elaborate?" I gritted out.

His eyes, identical to mine, slid my way. "What do you want to know?"

Jesus, he had me. I'd been acting like I didn't care, that walking away from her was no big deal. He knew I was full of it, though. Why the hell did I even bother trying to pretend otherwise? "Everything," I rasped, giving up all pretense of not caring. "Tell me everything."

My brother's eyes softened, and I hated it, hated that he could see how much this was killing me, because it would hurt him just as much to see me this way. That's just how we were.

He sat forward. "I saw her outside the library. She'd just finished for the day."

My fingers curled at my sides. "How did she look?"

"Pretty," Beau said. "She was wearing these jeans with butterflies and shit at the pockets, and a fluffy blue sweater. All that beautiful dark wavy hair of hers was loose down her back." He took a pull of his beer and levelled his eyes back on me. "And sad, Hank. She looked like she'd lost someone she loved."

I jerked back. "What?"

"There was no way to miss it, the pain she was feeling,

but there was a split second when she first spotted me, just a moment, where I knew she thought I was you…and, brother, she lit up like a sunrise."

I gripped one of the porch railings. "You talked to her?"

"She asked after you, wanted to know how long I was in town and if I could swing by her place before I headed home." He motioned to the cake. "She rushed home and baked that for you. Wanted me to drop it off."

I looked at the cake. Chocolate. She remembered how much I liked it. How my grandmother used to make me one every birthday.

"Think it'd only be polite to thank her in person, don't you?" Beau said.

I looked at my brother. "I don't know, I can't—"

"She's leaving, Hank."

My knees nearly buckled. "What?"

Beau leveled me with a look that made my gut clench painfully. "She was in the middle of packing."

No.

"She's not Mom," Beau said, and shoved his fingers through his hair. "Birdie's hurting. She cares about you. Christ, I think she might love you." He shook his head. "That makes you the luckiest bastard I know. I'd give anything for that, for a good woman like Birdie."

I straightened. I'd never heard Beau talk like that. "But she's leaving…"

"Ask her to stay," he said.

I stared at Beau, still trying to recover from the eighteen-wheeler this news had just driven through my chest, but my brother hadn't finished.

"You're not the only one who has shit they're dealing with because of Mom, and it's taken me a long time, a lot of wrong turns, to work out what I want. And, Hank, if you don't go to her and tell you how you feel, if you don't stop her from getting in her car and driving away, that would also make you the dumbest bastard I know."

"What if she leaves anyway?" I said, voice like nails on rusted tin.

Beau held my stare. "What if she doesn't?"

Birdie

I stood at the bathroom counter and looked at my pale reflection.

How long would it take for this not to hurt so much, for me not to miss him like something vital had been torn out of me?

As every day passed I was more convinced that there would never be relief from it. I loved him. That didn't just go away. It might fade in time, but I knew with everything in me that I would always feel this way.

Staying in this town, having him close...I couldn't do it anymore. I had to go.

I finished washing my face, patted it dry, and pulled my hair band out, letting my hair fall loose.

Did he like the cake? Was he eating it now?

Was he thinking of me?

I knew he liked to be alone, but the thought of him in that house all by himself—I hated it. I worried that he might be lonely, if he was taking care of himself, if he was eating properly. Ridiculous. The man had been taking care of himself all his life. He certainly wasn't starving himself. He didn't need me.

Still, I'd made the damned cake, my way of saying goodbye, I guess. I wanted to do something that would make him happy, maybe even put a smile on his face.

Let him know I cared.

I weaved around the boxes stacked in the hall, into my bedroom, and changed for bed. The long-sleeved white thermal top had blue polka dots and was long, hitting mid-thigh. I never bothered with PJ bottoms when I wore it—they only twisted during the night and made me crazy.

It wasn't late, but I was tired since I hadn't been sleeping much lately. I knew I'd still end up staring at the ceiling all night, but I had to try and get back into a routine. My old routine, before Hank.

I headed to the kitchen and grabbed a glass out of one of the boxes on the counter.

There was a knock at the kitchen door.

I spun toward it, my hand flying to my chest.

The door was half wood, half clear glass. It was at the back of the house, so I'd never really worried about it.

Standing on the other side of the window, one hand to the doorframe, head close to the glass, eyes locked on me...was Hank.

Oh God.

I was moving across the room before my brain fully registered.

I flicked the lock and yanked open the door.

"You're leaving?" he said on a harsh whisper.

"Hank..."

He stepped forward, colliding with me, and my words stalled in my throat when his arms banded around me and he buried his face against the side of my throat.

My heart pounded against the back of my ribs as I listened to him breathe deep.

"God, I missed you so damn much," he said against my skin, his big body trembling against mine. "Can't think, can't eat, can't fucking breathe without you." His lips brushed my neck. “Need you, Birdie, need you so bad. You can’t, you can’t leave me.”

My hand went to the side of his face. “I need you, too.” His head lifted, mouth seeking mine as I did the same. His tongue thrust past my lips, tangling with mine, and there was a desperation, an urgency, that made my head spin.

His big, rough-skinned hands dropped to my ass and his fingers slid up under my shirt then down the back of my underwear. “Need inside you, sweetheart. Christ, I’ll die if I don’t get inside you.”

He kept moving until my back hit the wall.

“Then take me,” I said, my voice as raw with need as his.

He moaned and tugged on my underwear, shoving them down my legs. As soon as they were off, his hand slid between my thighs, cupping me. “Pussy’s so wet, Birdie, so wet and hot for me.”

“Yes,” I said as my hands dropped to the front of his jeans and I tugged at his belt, undoing it then popping the button. I nipped his lower lip then sucked it as I slid down the zipper and freed his iron-hard erection. “God, I need you.”

His breathing was hard, harsh. Each breath came out as a gasp, pitched high, like he was fighting to control his emotions. He lifted me off the ground, and my legs came around his waist. Then he was there, his body pressing into me, every bit of his heat, his scent surrounding me.

He slammed up inside me, filling me in one hard thrust.

His mouth came back to mine and I fed him my scream of pleasure. He stayed deep, twisting his hips, grinding into me, causing a nonstop assault deep inside and against my clit all at once.

“Sweetheart,” he said against my lips. “Oh fuck, sweetheart.”

My whole body jolted as my orgasm exploded through me. I sunk my nails into his shoulders and sucked his lips, his tongue, trying to pull him closer when that was impossible. "God, I love you, I love you so much," I cried out, unable to keep it in any longer.

Hank made a sound like a tormented animal, then he growled, pulled out, slammed back in, and came hard inside me. My name flew from his lips and echoed around my small kitchen.

He glided in and out of me until the last pulse of his cock, until the last wave of pleasure rolled through us both. He kissed my jaw and lifted his head.

His gorgeous blue eyes bore into me. "You...you love me?"

I could try and backtrack. I could pretend it was the heat of the moment. We'd only known each other for such a short time. But I knew how I felt, and I realized I didn't want to take it back.

"Yes," I said. "And when you dropped me off and drove away, I didn't know how I was going to survive it. I still don't." I held nothing back.

"I never thought, after my mom left, after seeing my dad suffer through that..." He let out a shuddering breath. "I thought I did something wrong, that somehow it was my fault she didn't love me enough to stay, that I wasn't..." He shook his head. "I...I never thought I could be enough, enough for anyone. God, for someone like you."

My heart was breaking for him. How could he think that? "Hank—"

His eyes flared. "Say it again, Birdie."

I cupped his face, his beard tickling my palms, and held his desperate stare. "I love you, Hank Smith," I whispered. "So much."

A breath shuddered through him. "I love you, too, sweetheart. Christ, more than I thought was possible. I don't want to spend another night without you."

I shook my head. "Me either. I couldn't bear it."

He dipped his face, bringing it even closer to mine. "But can you...can you give it all up to be with me? Can you be happy in the mountains...with me?"

I smiled, unable to control the joy filling me. "It doesn't matter where I am. As long as I'm with you, I'll be happy."

His eyes searched mine, and there was fear there, fear that he couldn't hide from me.

"Hank, what is it?"

He gripped me tighter. "Promise me, if you need more, if you're not happy, promise you'll talk to me first, that you won't just leave me. Promise me that."

"I promise," I said, making sure he heard the truth in those words. "I've never had a home, not a real one. And being with you, Hank, you *are* home. You're what I've been searching for my whole life. Why would I ever leave that, leave you, now that I've finally found you? It's not going to happen. That will never happen."

He growled and carried me down the hall toward the bedroom. "Tell me you love me again."

"I love you."

He dropped me onto the bed and covered me. "Again," he rasped.

I slid my hand up the side of his throat, pulling him closer, and said against his lips, "I love you."

"Birdie," he said in a way that lifted goosebumps over my skin. "I'll work every day to make sure you're happy. Whatever you want, whatever you need, I'll—"

"Hank," I said.

He looked down at me.

"I've got you. I already have everything I want and everything I need. Love me and I'll be the happiest girl in the world. That's all I need."

He buried his face against my throat again, and then he made love to me until the sun came up.

EPILOGUE

FIVE YEARS LATER

Birdie

THE SOUND of sweet little girl giggles filled the living room, followed by Hank's deep voice and his soft chuckles.

As always, hearing my husband with his girls got to me. There was no sound I loved more.

I quickly put the last of the chocolate frosting swirls on the cake and turned to face them just in time. Hank rounded the corner, a grubby four-year-old on each shoulder.

I grinned at Beth and Emmy, giving the twins a little nod, and they both yelled, "Happy Birthday, Daddy!"

A huge smile spread across Hank's face before he dropped to one knee, lowering his daughters to the floor. The girls threw their arms around his neck, planted a wet kiss on each cheek, then released him and rushed me for a piece of cake.

"Daddy has to blow out his candles before we eat cake!" I said.

They squealed and clapped their hands as Hank moved in closer and I lit the candles. He dutifully blew them out, then I lit them again twice more so the girls each had a turn as well.

We all ate cake, and after a bath, Hank read them a story —and like always, fell asleep as soon as the girls did. I walked in to find him in the armchair, Beth and Emmy asleep in his lap and draped over his chest.

I gently shook his shoulder, and he opened his eyes.

"Let's get the girls to bed," I said and picked up Beth. Hank did the same with Emmy, and we put them to bed, pulling the door closed behind us.

I took his hand and led him down the hall to our room. "I had a surprise for you, but I think you might be too tired."

His arms came around me from behind and he lifted me off the floor. I stifled a squeal, but couldn't hold back my giggle as he dropped me on the bed and came down on top of me.

"I'm not too tired for my surprise," he growled against my ear.

He grew hard against my leg and I shivered. "You sure about that?"

"Positive."

"I'm wearing something special for your birthday," I said, sliding my hand down the front of my robe.

Hank's eyes flared, and his gaze dropped down to my chest. "Show me," he rasped.

"I thought you might like to unwrap me."

He licked his lips and I felt his heart pounding against mine. In five years, the only thing that had changed between us was that our love had grown stronger. We couldn't get enough of each other, and I knew that would never change.

He slid his hand down my front, tugged the belt free, then slowly, so damn slowly, opened each side.

"Birdie," he rumbled in that gritty way that made me wet and hot.

"I'm wearing my birthday suit just for you."

"I see that," he rasped. "And you're so damn beautiful, sweetheart." He kissed my bare skin, my chest and my belly. He sucked a nipple into his mouth and I arched, a moan escaping. "All mine."

I cupped his face and he looked down at me, eyes so hot and filled with want my breath burst past my lips. I dragged my thumb over his whiskered jaw. "What did you wish for?"

"Hmm?"

I threaded my fingers with his. "When you blew out the candles."

"I didn't," he said, then pressed his mouth to mine and moved his hand down my body, lower, spreading my thighs.

I shivered again. "Why not?"

He pressed hot, wet kisses over my breasts, my belly, and lifted his head. "I don't need to make wishes. I've got everything I ever dreamed of. The woman of my fantasies, who I love more than life, and our two beautiful girls. Birdie, there's nothing else I want."

My eyes welled with tears. "Love you, Hank."

"Love you, too, sweetheart."

Then there were no more words.

THE END

Thank you for reading Mountain Man!

Beau's story is up next in
WILD MAN
(The Smith Brothers #2)

The first time I saw Beau Smith's face, I fell for him... hard. There's just a few tiny problems. He lives wild. I've never left the city. He wants a wife who can handle his harsh world. I just want him.

He's been burnt in the past, and he won't let me in easily, but there's no denying the spark between us, so intense it could set the woods on fire. And with every hot and dirty night we spend together, I can feel his walls crumbling.

But once he realizes I'm not what he signed up for, that I lied to him about who I am—will he still want me, or will I lose my wild man forever?

If you're in the mood for more heroes like The Smith Brothers, larger than life with a heart of gold, you could try Elijah from Breaking Him.

Or Hugh from Swerve (Boosted Hearts #1)
Keep turning for an excerpt of chapter one!

I'd love to hear what you thought of Mountain Man. If you have a few moments to leave a review, I'd be incredibly grateful.

ALSO BY SHERILEE GRAY

The Smith Brothers:

Wild Man

Lawless Kings:

Shattered King

Broken Rebel

Beautiful Killer

Boosted Hearts:

Swerve

Spin

Slide

Axle Alley Vipers:

Crashed

Revved

Wrecked

Black Hills Pack:

Lone Wolf's Captive

A Wolf's Deception

Stand Alone Novels:

Breaking Him

ABOUT THE AUTHOR

Sherilee Gray is a kiwi girl and lives in beautiful New Zealand with her husband and their two children. When she isn't writing sexy, edgy contemporary romance, searching for her next alpha hero on Pinterest, or fueling her voracious book addiction, she can be found dreaming of far off places with a mug of tea in one hand and a bar of Cadburys Rocky Road chocolate in the other.

To find out about new releases, giveaways, events and other cool stuff, sign up for my newsletter!

Connect with Sherilee via Facebook, Instagram, Twitter or Pinterest.

www.sherileegray.com

SWERVE

BOOSTED HEARTS #1

CHAPTER ONE

Shay Freestone cursed her ridiculous, flimsily made Poison Ivy costume for the gazillionth time when Batman stepped in front of her, blocking her exit and fingered one of her leaves. She slapped away the creep's hand.

Kayla owed Shay big time for this. Her best friend had shoved her into the embarrassing ensemble two hours ago, quoting Section Two, Item Four of their Best Friends' Handbook, drafted when they were in the seventh grade, after Shay refused to go to the school dance— which meant they both didn't go—and in her friend's absence, Rob Dunkirk, the love of Kayla's life, had danced with April Gunson the entire night. The section in question stated that Shay Freestone and Kayla Green agreed to do whatever necessary, *whenever* required, in the pursuit of securing love for either of the aforementioned.

But *this*, this was going above and beyond.

Batman moved closer, a bead of sweat sliding down his

temple from under his now askew black mask. "Come on, Ivy. Don't go yet. The party's just getting started."

Gag. She tried to slip by, but he kept coming until his protruding belly—which was straining his utility belt dangerously—bumped into her, forcing her back a step.

"I really have to go."

He licked his fleshy, cherry-red lips and leaned in. "First, I need to find out if your kiss really is poisonous."

Is this cretin for real? She leaned back farther. Why on earth had she let Kayla drag her to this ridiculous party? Best Friends' Handbook, be damned. So what if Shay'd been a hermit the last few months? That was preferable to standing in a corner by herself the whole night, feeling like a complete idiot, while her traitorous friend, *in the pursuit of love*, was probably getting naked with Wolverine—aka Kayla's ex-boyfriend, James, and the reason she and Shay were here — back at his place. The couple had disappeared a little while ago. Her friend had bailed on her. Again. Kayla had conveniently forgotten *that* section of the blasted handbook. Now Shay was stranded without her wallet, phone, or the keys to her trailer since she'd stashed them in her friend's bag.

Maybe her gran had given a spare key to Edna next door? The pair had been thick as thieves before her grandmother passed away and left the place to Shay.

Batman's heavy breathing cut through her thoughts. His fingers moved lower. "So tell me, are you a natural redhead?"

Ew! She gave his hand a slap-shove combo. "I don't think —" "How about we go upstairs, and you let me find out?" *Oh, dear God.* Shay ducked under his arm, but he still had hold of the leaf on her costume,

and she felt it tear free as she made a dash for the door.

"Hey! Hold up. Wait for me," the idiot called after her. Shay shoved open the door and burst out onto the street, the cool, LA midwinter breeze

hitting her bare skin, seeping through the cheap fabric from all sides. She sucked in a startled breath. Her coat was also in Kayla's car. So not only did Shay have to walk home in the cold in a Poison Ivy costume with half her butt hanging out, she had to walk home in a *cheap*, crappily made Poison Ivy costume with missing leaves that, thanks to Batman, was now falling apart at the seams and losing more by the minute.

Speaking of The Caped Crusader, he stumbled out of the apartment building, spotted her and started in her direction. Fast... Faster than she would have thought possible with the sway he had going on.

She'd had her fill of creeps, enough to last her a lifetime. She didn't need this right now, dammit.

Okay, there'd only been one creep, in particular, but his creep factor had been abnormally high... So high, the guy easily equaled, like...a thousand creeps, at least. Not-so-old hurt and embarrassment reared up, hitting her in the face, heating her skin to excruciating levels.

Having a fling with your boss was stupid enough. Period. But having an affair with your boss then having to quit that job because you overheard him bragging and mocking you to his buddies around the water cooler, was a whole new level of mortification. Not to mention the hit to her bank account. Her two part-time jobs and the occasional graphic design gig she managed to pick up barely covered living costs, let alone the debt left by her grandmother. She'd been forced to take out a loan, using the trailer her gran had left her as collateral.

She slammed the door on those thoughts as quickly as they came. *Not now.*

Spinning on the heels of her boots, Shay speed walked down the street. There weren't many people around, but enough she was thankful for the thick green pantyhose she had on, which hid a goodly amount of cellulite and were tight enough to provide a small amount of wobble control.

The idiot behind her kept coming, calling out for her to, "Wait up."

Like heck.

With her only thought to lose him and get home as fast as possible, she ducked down the next street.

Only it wasn't a street, it was more an alley-slash-parking lot. Cars surrounded her, filling the reserved parking spots for the expensive-looking restaurant beside it. *Crap.*

She spun around as the Dark Knight rounded the corner, blocking the exit. "Ivy, why are you running from me?"

She backed up until she bumped into the car behind her. The cold steel chilled her, lifting goose-bumps all over her skin. The guy wasn't overly tall, but he was heavily built and kind of intimidating. She expected the car alarm to start wailing instantly—the vehicles parked around her looked high end, like sports cars and, um...stuff like that—but no such luck. Screw it all. The damn thing stayed silent.

She held up her hands to ward him off and shook her head. "All right. The fun's over. Why don't you head back to the party?"

He kept coming, licking his over-abundant red lips until they shone like candy apples; only these were gross, icky candy apples she seriously did not want to taste. The fool kept up the Batman persona, clutching the ends of his cape, lifting it up and down like wings. "I've come for my kiss, Ivy."

"If you come any closer..." He came closer. "Back up. *Now*." "Just one kiss."

"No." "Yes." He puckered up, crowding her. "No!" She gave him a shove... Gravel scraped behind her, loud enough that Batman heard it, too. He stopped his descent,

lifting his head. She watched the guy's eyes go wide, jaw unhinging. The sound of boots moving closer came next and had her whipping around to see who it was. She gaped like a dying fish.

A huge mountain of a man rounded the trunk and walked right up to them. He stared down at the creep in front of her and growled, "You got ears?" *Yes, growled*. Like a lion, or a bear, or

some other wild beast. Batman stared up at the man, slammed his mouth shut, looked at her, then back at the

mountain. "Um...y-yes?" "So you heard the lady tell you 'no'," her rescuer said, his eyes going kind of wild and

scary. "Well...um...I..." Batman was suddenly at a loss for words. He also seemed to have

sobered up rather quickly, the glazed look gone from his beady eyes. The mountain crossed his muscled arms, heavy biceps straining the sleeves of his faded

black tee, veins bulging along his corded forearms in a rather interesting way. Then, with his eyes still locked on his target, he said quietly, "Go."

His voice sounded soft and rough all at the same time, and set off some serious tingles— like, they were doing a high-energy gig up and down her spine. No, he hadn't shouted the word, but there was no mistaking the danger behind the order.

Batman finally snapped out of his stupor and started

backing up, nodding rapidly. As soon as he hit the entrance of the parking lot, he spun on his boots and sprinted away, cape flying out behind him from the sheer velocity of his escape.

The mountain watched the creep go, then his head swiveled on his muscled neck, and he dipped his chin so he was looking at her. "All right?" he rumbled.

Holy Hell. Her belly flipped. The guy was kind of terrifying. He was also extremely handsome in a scary, rough, mountainous kind of way. His hair was a little shaggy, and he had a full beard, but it wasn't the Grizzly Adams, shaggy kind of beard; it was trimmed and neat and suited the heck out of him. He was also *tall.* So tall, she was a good couple of inches shorter than his shoulder.

His dark brown eyes, which were surprisingly warm and kind, and ringed with thick, black lashes, locked on hers. "You okay, babe? He hurt you? You look kinda freaked."

Babe? Eeek. Her nether regions did a highly inappropriate but extremely happy little quiver at that deep, gruff voice. Which was crazy, because not only was she usually shy around men— especially attractive ones—but this guy was so far from her type it wasn't funny. "Ah...yes, I mean, no. I mean, I'm fine...now. T-thanks to you. You know...for coming to my rescue." *Jeez, spit it out.* She sounded as if she had a serious speech impediment.

"No problem." He stared at her for a few seconds, as if he was waiting for something. When

she didn't say or *do* anything, because she couldn't move, let alone make her mouth work, he added, "Think you're good to go. Guy's long gone."

"Um..." She stayed rooted to the spot, gaze fixed on the hulk in front of her. Bizarrely, it wasn't fear keeping her in place...it was that she was struggling to leave the big man's orbit; his gravitational pull was that strong.

What the heck is wrong with me?

His lips quirked up, just a little on one side, then those stunning eyes did a full-body sweep. The quirk turned into a grin. "What's with the outfit?"

Her face heated instantly. She'd almost forgotten she was wearing the stupid costume. She stared down at herself and cringed. Her wobbly bits were all on full display—butt, thighs, belly, boobs. *Perfect*. "I was at a...a costume party."

"What're you?" Her face got hotter. "Poison Ivy." He frowned, brow scrunching in obvious confusion. "She's a villain. Batman's nemesis...in a comic book." He kept his gaze locked on her, and his eyes started dancing. "Right." He was more than likely laughing at her, but right then, she didn't care; that sparkle in his

eyes just made him more appealing. Again, her reaction was completely insane. The men she usually found herself attracted to were business types—they wore suits, were clean shaven, were...*smaller*. Less imposing. But the scary, hard gaze he'd wielded like a weapon was long gone now. In fact, she felt safe standing there with him.

Without realizing what she was doing, she shuffled a little closer, drawn by that magnetic pull that seemed to surround him. He also looked warm and snuggly, and now the excitement had past, she was starting to feel the cold.

He watched her, something moving over his features, something that got those inappropriate tingles riled up all over again. Her hair rested over her shoulder, and he reached out, touching it with his index finger, as if he was testing her reaction.

"I like the hair."

"It's real," she blurted for some stupid reason, probably

because of Batman's lewd suggestion that the carpet didn't match the drapes. Not that she wanted this guy to see her carpet. No, that would be wrong, wouldn't it? They'd only just met.

He continued to stare at her, eyes still dancing in that highly attractive way. He also didn't answer, so she babbled on in an attempt to explain herself.

"I mean, it's not part of the costume. Though, Ivy does have red hair...it's just...it's not a wig." Then, out of nowhere and just to make her humiliation ten times worse, she added, "I like your beard."

Okay. She had no idea why she gave in to the urge to share that. She dropped her gaze to his big black boots, to hide the fact that the temperature of her face had skyrocketed by at least a thousand degrees.

"You do, huh?" His voice was rougher now, and God, the sexiest thing she'd ever heard.

She glanced up. His grin was wider, a full-blown smile. *Wow*. He looked good smiling. Like, *really good*.

"You want a ride some place?"

She blinked up at him. "Um..." For some crazy reason, she wanted to say yes, she wanted to go with him, this complete stranger, this huge, bearded, mountain man. "I, ah, I can walk. It's not that far."

His brows drew together. "How far's not far?" "Just a few blocks." *More like a million*. His brown eyes did another sweep of her body, and she shivered. "You're practically naked. It's cold"—his gaze went to her hands—"you got a phone?" "My friend accidentally took my things when she left the party." "She bailed on you?" Why was she telling this total stranger she had no money and no phone...was essentially

stranded? She had no idea. Still, she answered. "Yes."

"I'll give you a ride." There was no question in his voice this time. "Oh, no. I couldn't..." He moved to the next car along and opened the passenger door. "Yeah, you could." Then he looked her in the eyes, and what she saw made her tummy...and lower...melt

deliciously. "Babe, you're in no danger from me. Just don't like seeing assholes fuck with innocent

women. Brings out my grumpy side." For some crazy reason, she trusted him. Heck, she wanted to get into the car with him.

Maybe she was more her mother's daughter than she wanted to believe, because she said, "Okay," the word popping out of her mouth before she could think better of it.

His smile returned, wide and yummy, straight white teeth surrounded by sexy beard, and her heart did an erratic thump.

He motioned to the open car door. "Let's go."

Made in the USA
Monee, IL
15 January 2023